PRAISE FOR KICHO & NOB[illegible]

Is there a place for love in this turbule[illegible] endure? It retells the legend with intelligen[illegible]d dark, addressing affairs of honour and reven[illegible], intertwined with moments of sexual tension and [illegible] *[illegible]beth Beattie, writer, Making Sense)*

T0106235

This story is a heady mix of passion and politics. The author has broken new ground by making a woman the character, for feminine roles are underplayed in Japanese history. The story is enriched with details of Japanese politics and life which bring the time and the events vividly to life before the reader. *(Wendy McDonald, author)*

This charming and creative novel was written originally in Japanese and translated into English by the author herself. Amongst an abundant stories written in Japanese, only a handful are available in other language. The novel provides English readers with a rare and wonderful opportunity to experience the world of samurai of 16th century Japan. I wish that more Japanese stories are translated and read by English readers. It not only gives an enjoyment to the reader but also helps them understand the country of Japan which remains fairly isolated from the rest of the world. *(Yoko Pinkerton, author)*

A story of engaging charm! Nobunaga was an eccentric and powerful military commander who ran through the battle fields in the midst of provincial war period. Although he was said to have had 24 children, his relationships with his ladies were untold until the author's vivid imagination breathe life into Kicho, the wife of Nobunaga. This story also provides historical events involving Nobunaga with concision. *(Kei Knight, translator)*

Whilst Kicho and Nobunaga is a truly epic tale of a turbulent period in Japan's history, it is essentially a love story that reminds us that it is the human soul that shapes our history. Rumi's Nobunaga is both a hero and a tyrant, as lovable to some as he is fearsome to others. Whilst Kicho's desires are of the universal human heart—the need to love and be loved. Nobunaga's quest is to be the one to unify all the warring clans of Japan, while Kicho is determined to protect the man she loves—and often to protect others from him. While they both revel in victories and endure their losses, Nobunaga's on the battlefields and Kicho in the hearth, their love and destiny unfold together, often with a ruthless passion and without regret. Nobunaga and Kicho remind us that history is above all written from the heart. *(Anthony Davis, editor)*

Rumi Komonz

Copyright © 2011 by Rumi Komonz

All rights reserved. No part of this book may be used or reproduced by any means, graphic, electronic, or mechanical, including photocopying, recording, taping or by any information storage retrieval system without the written permission of the publisher except in the case of brief quotations embodied in critical articles and reviews.

Balboa Press books may be ordered through booksellers or by contacting:

Balboa Press
A Division of Hay House
1663 Liberty Drive
Bloomington, IN 47403
www.balboapress.com.au
1-(877) 407-4847

ISBN: 978-1-4525-0269-4 (sc)
ISBN: 978-1-4525-0270-0 (e)

Because of the dynamic nature of the Internet, any web addresses or links contained in this book may have changed since publication and may no longer be valid. The views expressed in this work are solely those of the author and do not necessarily reflect the views of the publisher, and the publisher hereby disclaims any responsibility for them.

The author of this book does not dispense medical advice or prescribe the use of any technique as a form of treatment for physical, emotional, or medical problems without the advice of a physician, either directly or indirectly. The intent of the author is only to offer information of a general nature to help you in your quest for emotional and spiritual well-being. In the event you use any of the information in this book for yourself, which is your constitutional right, the author and the publisher assume no responsibility for your actions.

Any people depicted in stock imagery provided by Thinkstock are models, and such images are being used for illustrative purposes only.
Certain stock imagery © Thinkstock.

Printed in the United States of America

Balboa Press rev. date: 11/30/2011

Forward

Oda Nobunaga was a brave samurai, an innovative politician and a successful businessman who ended the social upheaval of *Sengoku* period in 16c Japan. This is an untold story of his lady, affectionately known as the Princess of Mino (*Nohime)*. While the rest of Japan suffered constant military conflict, Mino, today's Gifu, where the princess's father ruled, had a busy market for fashion and foods.

In memory of Lady Oda Nobunaga, Kicho

Family Tree

= spouse | child + sibling

Lady Maki = Mitsutsuna + Mitsuyasu + Lady Omi **= Lord Viper** = concubine

Akechi Hide **Kicho**+Magoshio+Kiheiji+Toshiaki+Shingoro +**Yoshi=**Lady Ohmi

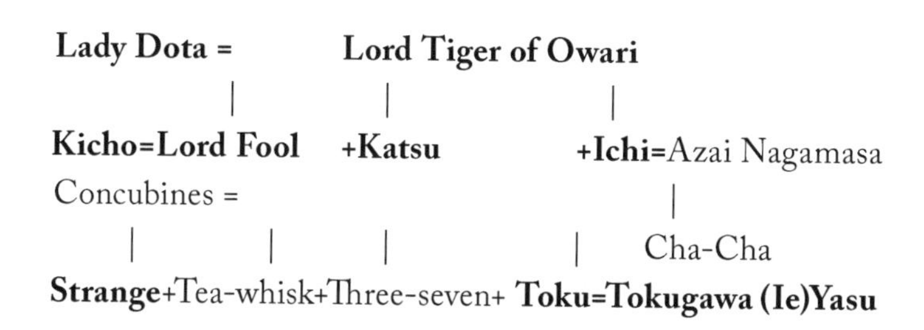

Main Characters

Kicho	Princess of Mino (Nohime). Lord Viper's daughter.
Lord Viper	Kicho's father. Lord Viper Saito Dosan of Mino.
Lady Omi	Mother of Kicho. Lord Viper's wife.
Hide	Kicho's cousin, Akechi Mitsuhide. Lived at the castle since childhood as a surety of the Akechis.
Lady Maki	Kicho's aunt. Hide's mother.
Brother Yoshi	Kicho's half-brother, Saito Yoshitatsu. Lord Viper's heir. His mother Miyoshino was the former Lord of Mino's concubine before she became Lord Viper's concubine.
Lord Fool	Oda Nobunaga
Lord Tiger of Owari	Oda Nobuhide, Kicho's father-in-law.
Lady Dota	Kicho's mother-in-law. Mother of Nobunaga, Katsu & Ichi.
Kano	Kicho's head maid from Mino. (fictional character)
Katsu	Kicho's brother-in-law, Oda Nobukatsu.
Oda Nobutomo	Nobunaga's uncle. Acting Lord of Owari.
Hirate	Nobunaga's retainer, Hirate Masahide.
Hotta	Lord Viper's retainer, Hotta Doku.
Hayashi	Brothers The Older Hayashi was Nobunaga's retainer and the younger was Katsu's.
Shibata	Katsu's retainer.
Sakuma Brothers	The Older Sakuma was Katsu's retainer and the younger was Nobunaga's.
Lord Strange	Oda Nobutada: Kicho's adopted son; Nobunaga's heir.
Toku	Adopted by Kicho, Nobunaga's eldest daughter who married Yasu's heir.
Ichi	Kicho's sister-in-law. Marries Azai Nagamasa
Saito Tatsu(oki)	Kicho's nephew. Saito Yoshitatsu's heir.
Ashikaga Yoshiaki	Lord Ashikaga Yoshiaki, Former shogun's younger brother

Events

*Daughter of Saito Dosan—Before 1548
*Proposal from Oda Nobunaga—autumn 1548
*To Owari—February 1549
*Fire at Kiyosu Castle—January 1551
*Girls' Festival—March 1551
*Funeral—March 1551
*Hirate's Torment—New Year 1553
*Father Meets Nobunaga—April 1553
*The Battle at Muraki Castle—January 1554
*Owari's Capital Kiyosu Castle—1554
*Lord Viper Saito Dosan's Bequest—April 1556
*Bon Dance at Tsushima Shirine—July 1556
*The Battle of Inou—August 1556
*The Battle of Okehazama—June 1560
*Kicho's Gifts of Abalones—September 1560
*Kiyosu Treaty (Toku's engagement)—February 1562
*Mount Komaki Castle—July 1563
*Ichi and Azai Nagamasa—1567
*Butterfly Returns—August 1567
*Gifu Castle—September 1567
*Shogun Ashikaga Yoshiaki—October 1568
*Nijo Castle—January 1569
*Lord Viper's Tea Pot—July 1569
*Mount Hiei—September 1571
*A Trophy—January 1574
*Peace Mound Azchi—1975
*Mitsuhide's Illness—April 1976
*Prime Minister Oda Nobunaga—November 1577
*Nene Visits Azchi—Spring 1579
*Aunt's Tragedy—July 1579
*Mitsuhide's Grandchildren—December 1579
*Horse Show—February 1581
*Kuwami temple—March 1581
*Exhibiting Azchi Castle—January 1582
*Tokugawa Ieyasu Vists Azchi—May 1582
*Honno Temple—June 1582

The stall sold Nashi pears, persimmons, green tea and rice dumplings. Other stalls sold kimonos, armours and swords. There was a smell of grilled prawns in the air.

"Isn't Princess Kicho the most beautiful thing you've ever seen?" said a young samurai.

"She is exquisite," said another. "Hush, there are dirty looking boys that we haven't seen before . . ."

A peasant boy in the vicinity whispered to another,

"Someone is following us."

"Money is handy. You can buy anything with it." His tall friend threw a prawn in his mouth and wiped his hands on the younger boy's humble kimono shoulder.

"Please remember. We are in the enemy territory."

"Don't worry," said the taller boy with a peasant style ponytail sticking up to the air.

"Old Hirate is negotiating a peace treaty."

He looked up at the castle standing tall at the top of Mount Kinka. He then turned to walk away in long strides. Under the shade of a large Gingko tree with yellow leaves, a samurai waited with three impressive horses. When he saw the peasant boys, he stood and bowed to the taller boy. The three horses trotted along the highway leading to the neighboring province Owari. When they came to the outskirts, the taller boy started to gallop. The other two chased, but the first horse soon went far ahead and disappeared in the woods.

*

Cherry Blossom

Princess Kicho in her embroidered silk kimono was walking among cherry trees in full bloom. A young samurai whispered,

"Princess."

He held something white in his hand. Thrusting it to her, he blushed and then he disappeared. It was a piece of paper which said,

"Allow me to visit you, tonight."

Princess Kicho, who had her first period recently, went straight to her father. The young samurai's face turned white. Did he fear that he was to be boiled alive, or ripped apart by oxen walking in opposite directions? Kicho's father, a prominent warlord in sixteenth century Japan, living in the imposing castle at the top of Mount Kinka, was the Lord Viper of Mino.

To the young man's great relief, however, Lord Viper didn't even yell at him. Since then, many Mino's samurai had given her love letters. One day, Kicho showed off yet another letter to her father, when her eyes met her cousin Hide's.[1] Twenty-one year old Hide was a resident

[1] Hide (pronounced Hidé)=Mitsuhide=あけちみつひで＝明智光秀

samurai since the age of eight, working for Lord Viper. Kicho decided to tease him.

"When are you going to give me a letter, Hide?"

A deep blush spread across Hide's neck. He used to think that Kicho, who followed along behind Lord Viper, was like his little sister. Recently, however, he saw her almond-shaped eyes sparkle in a way that he had never seen before. Since that day, Hide only had to hear her voice to feel aroused. The only problem was that it seemed indecent regarding his lord's daughter. Furthermore, he thought,

I am too proud to be ignored.

His thoughts, however, began to change.

My lord values me more than any other.

He imagined intimate moments with Kicho, fondling her long black hair. On the days he saw her up close, his heart would be filled with happiness all day. If he didn't see her for a few days, he would feel empty. If he saw her from a distance, or heard her rippling, wave-like voice, it was enough to make his heart pound.

*

A few months later, Hide met with his mother, Lady Maki.

"Our lord trusts you so much that he may give Princess Kicho's hand to you in marriage."

Lady Maki, who had married into the prestigious Akechi clan from the famous Takeda clan both with connections to the shogun's family, did not imagine that Lord Viper would allow Kicho to choose her own husband.

"I am . . . aware of that, dear Mother," Hide said. "But, if I married Princess Kicho, I would become an enemy to the young lord, Yoshi, the successor of Lord Viper."

"Yoshi was born seven months after the previous lord had given his concubine to Lord Viper . . ."

"Many believe that Yoshi's true father is the previous and rightful lord of Mino who Lord Viper displaced. They demand Lord Viper's early retirement as Yoshi has turned twenty. I don't want to be a rival to him by teaming with Lord Viper and Kicho's full-brothers."

"I understand. You are a considerate son. Let us drink to your future."

*

When Hide went outside, the pampas grass was dancing in the darkness. Hide crossed his arms in front and inserted his hands into his sleeves. A young woman stood gazing at him. It was not unusual for a woman to look at Hide in such a way. He was good looking, though slightly built. When three women gathered at the castle, they would love to talk about him. It was perhaps because he was deep in thought or maybe because he had drunk sake: Before he realized what he was doing, he found himself in the young woman's bedroom. He could recall her discreetly hiding his zori footwear from the public veranda . . . but he could not recall how he got into her warm futon.

The next morning, he regretted what he had done.

"Let us not see each other in this way again."

"You are a horrible man," Kano sobbed.

Because she did not stop crying, Hide found his zori himself. When he shut the sliding door, he could not hear her sob any more. He looked up at the eastern sky which was faintly crimson.

A few days later, Hide met Kano's tormented eyes. He thought of her soft breasts. They were generous, contrary to what he had expected from her skinny shoulders. His palms still remembered the feel of her nipples when they grew hard. Before he knew it, Hide stood in front of Kano's room that night.

The next morning, he regretted again.

"You are horrible." Kano sobbed.

"I am very sorry," Hide lowered his head. "I am in love with someone else."

*

In the autumn of 1548, Lord Fool's father Lord Tiger had a minor stroke and often felt numb in his limbs.

"I have managed to unite half of Owari in my life time. When I die, do not disclose my death for two years. I regret my son Lord Fool is too young at sixteen to guard the land from invaders. I do not want our peasants to suffer from battles ruining our precious land and crops."

"Certainly, my lord." Four men bowed simultaneously. They were Hirate, Hayashi, Shibata and Sasaki.

"Fortunately, the peace talks are progressing with Lord Tiger of Mino. We will endure until our young Lord Fool's adulthood," said Hirate, the chief lieutenant of Lord Tiger.

Shibata spoke next. "If young Lord Fool's behaviour does not improve, please consider his younger brother Katsu as your successor."

Lord Tiger slurred, obviously agitated.

"The Fool, is a mischievous kid, playing mock battles all day mimicing me. I've ordered you two to educate him properly!" He yelled at Hayashi and Hirate, who were Lord Fool's designated mentors.

"He trains with horses every morning and evening; he's the best swimmer in Owari. He practises archery, shot gun, and the art of war daily. However, his manners are . . ." Hayashi searched for words.

Hirate said, "Young Lord Fool is studying arts and manners at Tennobo Temple. Please allow a little more time, my lord."

Lord Fool's father nodded decisively.

*

It seemed that the number of peasant houses had increased recently in Owari. Suddenly, an incredible scream echoed across the width of the vast Nobi (Mino and Owari) plain.

"Go, go, go!"

Rag clad peasant boys came out of a bush. Each was holding an incredibly long bamboo stick—more than six metres long. From the opposite bush, a team of samurai boys holding bamboo sticks about the length of usual long spears rushed out. The two groups clashed. They seemed to know which team they belonged to by the way they dressed.

Up on the hill stood a boy, tall and slender, observing the way the two groups fought. The boy looked about sixteen; he had one shoulder bare tucking his short kimono under. He wore no hakama trousers, his long legs stuck out of his short kimono, the kind a peasant boy would wear. His ponytail, standing up to the sky, was tied with bright green strings—Did he think he looked cool this way?

"Stop!" he yelled. The two teams separated.

"Short spears are useless," he declared and gave the group with the longer sticks a huge bag full of persimmons. He then gave a bag of fruit to the other group as well.

*

When the boy returned to his castle covered with mud and dust, a man was waiting for him. The distinguished samurai with silver hair was Hirate.

"My young lord, do not dress like a peasant. Please do not hang on to your retainers' shoulders munching food as you walk. Your countrymen are calling you the Fool."

"Do I care?" said Lord Fool.

"I am afraid that the officials disapprove of your birthright to be the next lord."

"They will obey Father."

"Considering your father's ill health, may I suggest an alliance with Lord Viper of Mino, a prevailing kingdom next to our Owari?"

"I went to Mino the other day. They sell anything and everything at the *big* market. I heard the Viper's daughter is the most beautiful girl in Mino."

"Lord Viper went to Mino years ago as an oil merchant and stole the country from its powerless lord to build the wealthiest district in Japan. The market attracts merchants and shoppers from all over Japan."

"The Viper must be a genius. He who rules Mino rules Japan, they say. I want Mino; I want the Viper's daughter."

Hirate's jaw dropped. He was only trying to protect the young lord's humble succession rights in Owari. In the next moment, however, Hirate grinned. He realised that his young lord and he had the same immediate aim—a wedding with Lord Viper's princess.

"Listen, my young lord. Lord Viper loves the princess so much that he has refused every marriage proposal. You must improve your manners to be an eligible . . ."

Hirate breathed in to start a lecture.

Equally enthusiastic as Hirate, Lord Fool spoke first.

"The most beautiful girl in Mino is the beloved princess of the man who stole Mino. She has a prestigious Akechi blood line from her mother's side. Hirate, go to Mino and tell the Viper's daughter that I fell in love with her. Tell her that I don't want any other woman but her. Tell her that I will keep invading Mino until she comes to me—even if it costs my life."

"With this marriage, my lord," Hirate cried, "your future is secure."

**

It was a clear night with a full moon in Mino. Kicho and her cousin Hide went for a stroll in the garden at the castle after a moon-viewing gathering at Hide's mother's lounge. The moon was so bright, it was almost like daylight.

"Watch out, Princess . . ."

"Oh!" Kicho nearly tripped over a stone.

Hide quickly reached over and caught her kimono clad body. It had been many years since he held her like this. Contrary to Hide's fear, Kicho did not resist. She snuggled him as she used to do as a little girl.

I wish to be held tighter,

She was feeling insecure as there was a talk of her possible marriage to Lord Fool of Owari, a neighbouring province. As she knew she was expected to grow up, she hoped that Hide would show her the art of love.

Every young man in Mino adores me. Why not Hide? I am ashamed of myself for teasing him the other day. I just wanted to pretend I thought nothing of him.

"What a beautiful moon," Kicho looked at Hide.

"Isn't it? There's not a single cloud . . . by the way, Princess, I saw my foster-father yesterday."

"The lord of Akechi Castle?"

"He says I am now old enough to take over the position of the lord of the castle from him."

"You are the rightful lord of Akechi Castle, the first grandson of our grandfather."

Kicho was excited as she thought they had decided to make him the lord of the castle so that he could take her as his bride. She held her breath, almost choking.

"I replied, however, that I wish to keep working near Lord Viper."

"Will you please tell me why, Hide?"

"I like being close to you, Princess."

Hide loves me!

Kicho's head was turning hot; she tried to control herself.

"It is uncertain how long I am allowed to stay here at this castle, my dear Hide."

She prayed he would respond with courage.

"Are you going to marry Lord Fool?" asked Hide without a trace of emotion.

"Probably." Kicho was angry with Hide for her disappointment. Kicho turned to him but she could only see the outline of his face as the moon was directly behind him. He said,

"We'd better go back before our mothers start to worry, dear princess."

Hide gently took Kicho's hand and guided her along the pathway covered with pebbles so she wouldn't fall again. They didn't utter a word until they returned to his mother's lounge. The two ladies were nowhere in sight. A single lantern offered soft light. There was a fragrant smell of "ko" perfume. It was a cold night, but a warm futon was spread out. Hide realized that their mothers had intended to provide a romantic atmosphere for Kicho and himself.

How I wish to have an intimate moment with my princess.

The room was dimly lit, but he knew the way around his mother's room. "This way, please." He led Kicho to a private space draped with delicate materials made of silk. Kicho's kimono was heavy with the dew.

He helped her undress to an underwear kimono made of pastel-pink satin and tucked her into the warm futon. He then undressed also to a single layer of kimono. He came into the futon saying, "Allow me to warm you up." He rested next to Kicho, holding her hands. He then hugged her shoulders.

"I have loved you for a long time. I fear it may be a dream to be with you like this. Should it be a dream, I wish never to wake up."

Kicho was trembling, but whether she was feeling cold, was uncertain.

"Allow me to warm your feet." He held her feet between his thighs. He slid his hands gently along her face, shoulders, and breasts. He then kissed her. Kicho stopped trembling. Guided by Hide, she put her arms around his neck.

"How many times did I dream of you and I together like this?"

He closed his eyes and moved his head side by side to enjoy her hands on the back of his neck. Hide separated the front of her kimono to put his hand inside. He slid his fingers over her belly and further down, never letting his eyes off her face.

"Ah," Kicho gasped at the sensation she never knew before. Lit by the lantern, she looked like the little girl he used to know. He moved his fingers up and down, kissing her occasionally for assurance, monitoring her pleasure all the time. He continued this for a long time. Hide pushed Kicho's thighs with his knees and she felt something thicker and hotter than his finger. He kept his eyes on her. Dimly lit by the lantern, she looked too young to be a bride, for anyone.

Hide looked hurt whispering,

"I love you, my princess," he then moved no more. She felt something warm splash around her belly-button. He got up slowly. Wiping her lower abdomen carefully with kaishi paper, he said, "It is heartbreaking to think that the days may be numbered before I must part with you, forever."

"Please come to my room." Kicho's determined eyes glittered in the darkness. She needed to feel safe in Hide's arms for the rest of her life.

Allowing her fingers to entwine with his, Hide said, "Do I have your permission to stay with you for the night?"

Kicho squeezed his finger nodding desperately. She could not see his expression in part darkness and watched his shoulders sway as he breathed. She sensed his hesitation.

How I wish to keep my princess to myself, forever.

Hide marrying Kicho, however, would show the Akechi clan's ambition to rival young Lord Yoshi, by allying Kicho's full-brothers with the Akechi blood line. Akechi Castle was located near the border of Mino and Owari. If the peace talks with Owari failed, it would be the first castle to be attacked. Hide would not be able to expect a supporting force from Yoshi if he did not cooperate with him. He thought it would be a fatal mistake to go to her bedroom that night.

How can I explain all this to a fifteen year old princess?

Hide tried the best he could.

"My dear princess, I hope you forgive my behaviour tonight. I think of you as a precious little sister. I should not go to your bedroom. Rest assured you are still a virgin and please remember that I wish you all the happiness regardless who you marry."

"Thank you."

Tears gushed out of Kicho's eyes and she could not see a thing.

He does not want me? Can any man reject the most eligible woman in Mino, beloved princess of Lord Viper? I am not even engaged to Lord Fool: Why is Hide so cruel and speak as though I were Lady Fool?

Kicho was too young to ask such a question. The only thing she understood was that he rejected her sincere love. She hated Hide for the humiliation he caused and hated herself. *

Lord Viper sat on an embroidered silk cushion on tatami mats. He had his elbow on the arm rest made of black lacquered wood and silk padding. He was in his spacious lounge partitioned by hand-painted fusuma sliding doors. He made his presence felt even though he was not a large man.

"Did you," Lord Viper cleared his throat. ". . . sleep with Hide?"

As she swayed her head sideways, Kicho heard her long hair make a noise.

"Did Mother tell you that we went out alone after the moon-viewing party?"

Kicho looked at her father through her eye lashes. Her lips trembled.

"Good . . . Hide is an honest man, as I knew," Lord Viper did not enquire further.

Lord Viper took out something white out of the front layer of his kimono.

"This is from the Fool of Owari."

Kicho took the Mino paper in both hands.

"'Dear Princess Kicho of Mino'—A vigorous hand writing, isn't it, Father? . . . 'To cease strife or do strike . . . Time has come to be my wife,'" Kicho tilted her neck.

"What is this Father? A riddle?"

"A young man gives you a letter, what do you think it is?" Lord Viper giggled.

"Not romantic enough to be a love-poem . . . 'Time' is a homonym to the heritage of the Akechi clan. Does he mean he will attack Akechi Castle if I don't marry him?"

Kicho twisted her lips. She was wearing a Yuzen yarn-dyed silk kimono with hand-painted flowers in rainbow colours. Lord Viper looked at the garden and let out a deep sigh. He watched a camellia bush when a crimson flower dropped. Lord Viper squeezed out a voice.

"Will you go to Owari for me?"

"Of course, Father. It is my sincere wish to marry Lord Fool."

Kicho looked her father in his eyes. The heartache of lost love had not crushed her. It made her grow up.

Lord Viper looked at Kicho's almond eyes and blinked.

"The Fool has a younger brother called Katsu, a handsome young samurai." Knowing she liked a good looker, Lord Viper grinned at her, but only briefly.

"Unlike fierce Fool, who plays mock battles all day, gentle Katsu is well liked by his mother and his retainers. It is better for us also if Katsu, instead of the Fool, succeeded their father."

"Really?"

"You see, it will be easier for us to make Owari subordinate. Katsu lives with his parents at the main castle. When his sick father passes,

I am sure he will stay on as the successor. You shall be Katsu's wife, then. Is it clear?"

Kicho nodded.

Lord Viper took his treasured dagger out of his front kimono layers and placed it on tatami.

"You shall kill the Fool with this."

"He is a skilled swordsman, I believe," said Kicho as she took the dagger.

Lord Viper nodded.

"If he really is a fool, there will be an opportunity."

She fumbled the dagger in an exquisitely crafted embroidered case.

"What if I fall in love with him, Father?"

"Make sure you don't, my dearest Kicho."

Lord Viper bit his lower lip and looked away.

"If I do," said Kicho, uncasing the blade. "I may use this against you!"

Lord Viper lost his balance dislodging the arm rest. Kicho lifted her shoulders, chuckling.

Lord Viper laughed, wiping at his tears.

"I am *so* proud of you, Kicho! You certainly *are* the Viper's daughter! Young vipers are born tearing the mother viper's womb. Do not hesitate to overcome your father. You know that it is my paramount wish to end the civil war in Japan. The weaker should quickly obey the mightier to unify Japan to end the civil war before too many young men die."

"I shall never forget your wishes, Father."

When Kicho bowed, the smell of fresh straw of the tatami mats went straight through her nostrils.

*

When Kicho's engagement to Lord Fool Nobunaga was announced, Hide congratulated her with a gift of hand crafted mirror. It was made of polished silver with subtle bellflower, Akechi's crest design at the back. Kicho looked aside and said,

"I thought you were horrible, Hide."

Hide left Lord Viper's castle shortly after, to live with his uncle, the lord of Akechi Castle, as the successor in training. Lord Viper had given freedom to Hide, who had been at the castle since the age of eight as a surety, but, people who didn't know them well thought that Hide had fallen out with Lord Viper because the lord gave Kicho to someone else.

*

The castle was still in complete darkness. On a chilly morning in February 1549, Kicho climbed into the koshi[2] carriage, which Lord Viper had crafted for this day, lacquered red and decorated with tassels. When Lord Viper and Kicho's older brothers went outside, the sky was turning faintly purple. A father and his sons huddled together in the chilly wind, watching her koshi fade away in the morning mist covered the vast Nobi (Mino-Owari) Plain.

When Kicho's koshi crossed the border, four samurai boys walked over and bowed. Kicho pushed the small window of the koshi open.

With a neigh of a horse, a boy on horseback jumped out of a bush.

He looks exactly as I heard.

He demanded, "As we are now in Owari, do let us take the koshi."

His red undergarment showed inside the short kimono between his muscular thighs, as he wore no hakama. Kicho lowered her eyelashes.

Blinking nervously, Hotta, the man in charge of her procession ordered his men to lower the koshi. Lord Fool's retainers bowed and lifted the koshi. Once the koshi was on their shoulders, the four boys started to walk briskly.

They were so fast that the procession from Mino was soon left behind. Kicho's koshi did not head to the main castle as planned. Instead, it disappeared behind the stone walls of Lord Fool's Nagoya Castle.

Lord Fool's father, Lord Tiger of Owari, only grinned when he heard this.

---

2 a carriage carried by men 輿

"My Lord Fool knows that if his brother Katsu got hold of the princess, he will lose his right for succession and perhaps his life as well."

Lord Tiger accompanied Lady Dota to Nagoya Castle to meet Kicho.

"Welcome to Owari, dear Princess," said Lady Dota. "We had prepared for a reception at the main castle. I am sorry that Lord Fool snatched your koshi to bring you directly to Nagoya Castle. He has no manners. Did he frighten you?"

"Not at all Mother."

"I promise to have you at the main castle another time, dear princess."

*

Lord Fool did not come to Kicho's chamber on their wedding night. When it was still dark and Kicho was dreamy, she heard the wooden gate squeak. A high-pitched voice was heard outside and Kicho jumped out of her warm futon. When she got her maid to open the wooden sliding doors, she saw a boy dressed like a peasant. Sixteen year old Lord Fool was tall, but Kicho was used to seeing her giant half-brother Yoshi. Looking at Lord Fool's long legs sticking out of his short kimono, Kicho thought,

He's only a boy.

"You are perspiring like a horse, my lord."

"I've been training horses," said Lord Fool, rather boorishly. Lord Fool looked right into Kicho's eyes. She felt her face turn hot.

His eyes are like precious stones.

Lord Fool went into her chamber and stared at her collection of expensive furniture from Mino. Among them was an imposing kettle for a tea ceremony.

"I hear that your father stole Mino from the previous lord by befriending him through a tea ceremony."

Kicho looked at Lord Fool sternly.

"Tea ceremony is a popular art in Kyoto through which samurai and commoners can mingle."

"Can you show me how it's done?"

Kicho had her maids prepare. Lord Fool looked at Kicho's hands as they moved elegantly. Lord Fool's thirteen year old page, Juami waited in the garden with one knee on the ground. Juami twisted his lips as he looked at Kicho through his thick eye lashes. When he realized that Lord Fool's eyes were on him, however, he straightened his back.

Lord Fool ignored Juami.

"Charming," he said, but, after tasting the thick green tea, he frowned.

"How did you like it?"

Lord Fool slowly bent his handsome lips and said, "Bitter," but his eyes were smiling. The sun was already high up. The plum trees had plump buds about to blossom in the courtyard where the sparrows played.

*

Soon came the season of azalea blossoms. On a warm and humid day after lunch, Lord Fool said,

"You can ride a horse?"

"Yes!" Kicho was enthusiastic, but Kano, the head servant from Mino, shook her head. Kicho added, "Only if it is a calm one." Cheeks blushing, Kicho looked boyish with her hair tied and wearing riding trousers. Lord Fool's eyes sparkled when he saw her. "We are going to the river to teach Takechiyo how to swim."

Takechiyo was a six-year-old surety from neighbouring Mikawa province. By the time they arrived at the river, Kicho was perspiring on horseback. Lord Fool stripped bare before anyone else and jumped into the river. His younger retainers followed.

Each body is trim and full of muscles, more so than Hide or my brothers.

Lord Fool reached the other side of the bank before anyone else. The boys exclaimed with pleasure as they let Lord Fool piggy back on them. They would chase after Lord Fool as he got away.

Kicho was jealous. She undressed to a bathing robe and waded into the clear water. The soles of her feet felt slippery on the mud at the bottom of the river.

With a spurt of a dolphin, Lord Fool's head poked out of water.

"You can't miss a hot day like this. I swim from April to October."

"You can't swim in a robe . . ."

Kicho's bathing robe was already wet and stuck to her skin, showing her prawn colour nipples through. She crossed her arms in front.

Lord Fool looked up and said, "You'd better start swimming or you get chilly."

Kicho immersed herself in the water, remembering the time she swam with Hide and her brothers at her father's Sagiyama Castle's ornamental lakes as a little girl. Lord Fool had swum away to the other side of the river and his young retainers chased.

Lord Fool swam back to Kicho at a surprising speed. He grasped at Kicho. She giggled and splashed water at him. Lord Fool jumped on her back just as he did to the boys. Half of him being in the water, he was not too heavy. Kicho laughed and tried to elbow him off her back. Lord Fool's hand inadvertently brushed Kicho's breast. She took no notice and they playfully struggled. When Lord Fool's hand touched her breast for the second time, his hand stopped. He divided the front of Kicho's kimono to grab at her other breast. A sensation ran through her spine. She felt something move at her back.

"A frog!" she screamed, but Lord Fool grasped her tight. Lord Fool pressed his chest hard against her back, and she felt his heart beat getting faster like a war drum. Kicho felt the creature grew harder. It was not the gourd water bottle, which was left at the river bank.

"I'll sleep with you tonight." When a husky voice brushed Kicho's ear, a tickling sensation ran from her ear to the spine.

Takechiyo and his young retainers soon returned from the other side. As Kicho helped the boys squeeze water out of their clothes, her hands trembled. Boy's voices echoed in the sky. Butterflies fluttered here and there. Birds were chirping under the shade of the tree.

That night, Lord Fool called far away from the main quarter. "Kicho, come over here!"

She was embarrassed to be called to his chamber like a concubine. In Mino, Lord Viper discreetly visited Lady Omi's chamber.

This is a surprise attack of warfare.

When he saw Kicho coming, Lord Fool returned to his room. He then reappeared wearing a new white robe.

"Hirate says I ought to sleep with you."

He looked embarrassed. Kicho chuckled at her husband who used ever-serious Hirate to make an excuse.

*

Lord Fool surveyed his territory on horseback every morning and night. He gathered nearby farmers' sons to have mock fights. He trained them with much longer than usual spears. He also trained the gun squad. He never kept still. After making love, he was snoring lightly. His skin, which had been fair, became brilliantly tanned in summer. Under the soft light of lantern, Kicho watched him.

He smiles while he sleeps, like a kitten that has stolen a sashimi slice. He does not know he is sleeping with his assassin. I can slash his throat and no one will know . . . except for Juami who sits all night in the adjacent room.

Kicho scantly remembered her father's words, "We want Katsu to be the successor." She wondered what it would have been like with Hide, but only briefly. She placed her lips behind Lord Fool's large earlobes. Breathing quietly so she wouldn't wake him, she fell asleep.

*

When Kicho woke one morning, her maids looked worried.

". . . Lord Fool's pages were saying that Lord Viper's retainer Nagai sent a messenger that he is planning to assassinate Lord Viper . . ."

"Can't be. Nagai is also my half-brother . . ."

"Apparently, Nagai invited Lord Fool to take advantage of the turmoil."

I should let Father know, before it is too late!

Kicho's chief maid Kano rode a horse to Mino that morning. After a few days, Kano returned.

"Lord Viper interrogated Nagai, who then left him to work for your brother Yoshi."

"I hope I did the right thing by sending you to Mino. Father must feel lonely to lose me, Hide and now Nagai . . ."

Kicho shivered at the thought of a false rumour.

Father used the same tactic to disrupt the unity of his opponents . . .

When the maids were gone, Kicho took out her father's dagger from her breast layers of kimono. She fumbled the embroidered case. It had faint smell of Lord Viper.

I miss you, Father.

Kicho embraced the dagger at her breast. She took the dagger out of the case and inspected the sharp edge. She shook her head side to side and cried.

*

Kicho and Lord Fool had been married for nearly two years by 1551. On New Year's Day, he did not take a day off from his usual surveying on horseback.

"It is good that you have returned early, in time for the New Year's celebration." Kicho helped him to change.

"Smoky smell . . . where have you been?" Kicho looked at Toshi, fourteen year old page waiting out in the courtyard. When he rubbed his cheek, he smeared cinder all over his face.

There was a sound of someone running in the corridor and Hirate ran into the room.

"My lord, the fire . . . Kiyosu Castle is on fire!" Kiyosu was where Lord Fool's uncle lived.

Lord Fool was calm. "Shut all the gates! In case there is an attack from . . ."

". . . from Mino!" When he saw Kicho Hirate hastily bowed.

"I'll go and tell them to put the armour on," and off he went.

When Hirate was out of sight,

"You didn't, did you, blaming Father?" Kicho pulled Lord Fool's waistband with all her might. Losing his balance from a jerk, Lord Fool laughed,

"It was fun, wasn't it Toshi? Eight of us on horseback rushed over to the gate, and when they shut it we'd go around to another gate, throwing fire arrows inside stone walls and making lots of noise. We scattered our long spears everywhere before coming home."

"Long spears? The ones that you invented? They'll know the villain was you in no time . . . but . . . Why did you?"

Lord Fool turned serious.

"Do you think I am a fool? Everyone says I am and I don't care, but you are . . . my wife. Lord Fool looked away. "Perhaps I am asking too much."

"Only eight horsemen . . . and you let them know it was your doing?"

Lord Fool grinned.

"You wanted them to suspect there was another force within Kiyosu . . . to revolt with you, am I right?"

"Uncle Nobutomo is campaigning for Brother Katsu to be Father's successor. I'm not going to be bullied."

If his uncle intervenes in the succession right, Lord Tiger is gravely ill or may already have passed . . . but, why did Lord Fool tell me? He obviously trusts me more than his uncle. Does he trust me more than Hirate?

*

A few months later, Kicho received a parcel from Brother Yoshi who became the Lord of Mino after Father's retirement. It was an embroidered silk Kimono in cheerful spring colours. Delighted, she draped it over her shoulders when a small piece of paper fluttered onto the tatami. She scrunched it in her hand and sent her maids off for an errand.

A short message said, "Time to be Katsu's".

Fingers trembling, Kicho put the letter in hibachi[3] with burning charcoal. The paper turned into a flame. Gazing at it, Kicho remembered her father's words.

"We want Katsu to be the successor."

3 a large container used for heating and boiling water.

My husband's life is in danger.

Kicho poked at the ashes of the burned piece of paper in the hibachi with cold chopsticks made of brass. Ashes crumbled, making an eerie noise.

A few days later, on the Girls Festival day of March 3, 1551, Kicho was a guest of honour at Lord Fool's mother, Lady Dota's lounge in the main Suemori Castle.

"Let us celebrate with white sake," said Lady Dota as she poured a drink for Kicho.

"You are so kind, Mother."

"By the way, Kicho, are you with a child?"

"No, Mother, why?"

"I am relieved to hear that, my dear."

"Why, Mother? I envy you having many children."

"You are a good wife, Kicho. Too good for Lord Fool."

"Mother . . . ?"

"Though Lord Fool is my own son, he, who walks around munching food and hanging on retainer's shoulders, cannot be my husband's successor. My second son Katsu, by contrast, is well-mannered and trusted by all."

Poor Lord Fool surely wants his mother's love.

"Retainers agree that Katsu should be the successor."

"No . . ."

"Please, Kicho. You are an important princess from Mino. You should support Katsu for the sake of Oda family union."

Having had white sake, listening to Lady Dota, Kicho's head started to spin. She went to the adjoining room separated by fusuma sliding doors to rest.

Kicho woke in a futon with an excruciating headache. She saw a blurred figure of a neatly dressed young samurai. It was Lord Fool—in formal attire, complete with an articulate samurai hair style. Without a word, *that* Lord Fool lifted the futon doona and took Kicho's hand. The grip felt cold. Kicho tried to grasp the hand but was powerless. Did the white sake have something in it?

"You shall be my wife," a low voice said.

Refocusing her eyes, Kicho realized that he was Lord Fool's brother Katsu, who she saw in the hallway earlier. She panicked.

"Don't be rude," she tried to say, but her lips did not move. She tried to pull her hand away, but her entire body felt too heavy.

"Father has passed away. Mother and our retainers wish me to be his successor. I need you to live here at the main castle as my wife."

"Where is my husband?"

Kicho gasped, but not a word came out of her mouth.

Was he killed?

She felt a stream of tears run down the side of her face.

Everyone wants me to be Katsu's wife?

At that moment in the distance, a sharp voice quarrelled with Lady Dota.

"This way, my lord!"

The urging voice was Kano's. The loud sounds of footsteps approached.

"Please hurry . . ." Kicho tried to yell, but not a sound came out.

Katsu's face came closer as he tried to kiss her helplessly lying down in futon.

She gathered all her might in her teeth.

"Ouch . . ."

Katsu pulled away pressing his lips with bloody fingers.

"I cannot take this shrew as my wife."

Katsu got up, as the fusuma sliding door flew open.

"Away."

Kicho saw Lord Fool in his usual attire and closed her tired eyes. A thump was felt on tatami near her head. Lord Fool might have kicked Katsu to make him fall. Listening to the voices of Lord Fool and Lady Dota arguing,

"It had been decided," or

"She is *my* wife,"

Kicho drifted back into unconsciousness.

When she found herself in her own futon, Kano was sitting beside her.

"How are you feeling, my lady?" Her smile showed strain.

"Lord Fool carried you on his shoulder to his horse. He rescued you after defending Nagoya Castle from Lord Katsu's retainers' attack."

No wonder my body aches.

Kicho remembered Lord Fool's urgent voice,

"No time to wait for your koshi carriage . . . I'll put you on my horseback on your tummy . . . Can't you hold on? . . . O.K., I've got you . . . It's a rough ride, endure."

Kicho said to Kano,

"I was almost upside down on the horseback. It was scary . . . Lady Dota used the Girls' Day celebration as an excuse to invite me out to the main castle while Katsu sent military forces to take control of my lord's Nagoya Castle."

*

The funeral for Lord Tiger was on March 9, 1551. Katsu, Lady Dota and Kicho waited for Lord Fool's arrival at the temple, with the hall full of Lord Tiger's former retainers. The readings by priests had finished and the bell rang out.

Lady Dota fumed, "If he does not come to his father's funeral, he has no right to be the successor. We have no option but to have Katsu instead."

Katsu stood. Just then, Hirate yelled outside,

"Please, one moment!"

Lord Fool ran into the hall and pushed Katsu aside. Katsu put his hand to his small ceremonial sword, but changed his mind and stepped aside. Lord Fool not only had his long fighting sword but also wore his peasant-like attire. Dragging the hem of his long ceremonial hakama trousers, Katsu knew who had the advantage.

As Lord Fool proceeded, eyeing Katsu's retainers, the priests restarted the readings in chorus. At the next moment, Kicho put her hand on her mouth. Running up to the incense burner, Lord Fool grabbed a handful of incense pieces and threw them at his father's plaque. He then ran back out of the hall before anyone could utter a word.

"How rude can he be?" Lady Dota was furious, and the hall full of people seemed to agree, except Kicho.

If he had stayed, Katsu's supporters would not have missed the opportunity to get him. I am glad he got out of the hazardous zone quickly.

Kicho feared for bloody battles between the brothers, but, Lord Viper saved this critical situation. Hotta, who represented Lord Viper at the funeral, made it clear that Lord Viper supported Kicho's husband as the successor for Lord Tiger. The Mino-Owari border had been peaceful since Kicho's marriage to Lord Fool and no one wanted to upset Lord Viper, especially at this vulnerable stage after Lord Tiger's passing.

Thank you, Father.

Kicho put her palms together and bowed facing Mino.

**

After his father's passing, Lord Fool managed to hold on to his Nagoya Castle for two more years assisted by Hirate's diplomacy against Katsu's supporters.

During the New Year's party in 1553, Hirate demanded,

"You have turned twenty, my young lord. You should dress properly as a samurai."

"Why should I?"

"Make it a New Year's resolution."

"No."

"You have no idea how important it is to gain the respect of others."

Lord Fool refused and during a heated argument under the influence of sake, he kicked Hirate repeatedly.

Shortly afterwards, Hirate stood in Kicho's courtyard,

"I beg you marry Lord Katsu this year. All the retainers from the main Semori Castle support him and I can no longer control them."

"I said I will not. How many times do I have to say the same thing?"

Hirate looked down, and Kicho watched his shoulders tremble. When he looked up, she saw tears in his eyes.

"My lady, farewell and thank you."

Hirate went home and committed seppuku. He imposed on himself an honorable form of death penalty reserved only for a samurai.

*

Kicho was sleeping beside Lord Fool at their Nagoya Castle.

"Hirate!" A sudden outcry near her earlobe almost stopped her heart beat. A corner of the futon doona flipped to cover Kicho's face.

Did my lord have a nightmare?

Kicho pushed the futon slowly away.

Lord Fool was sitting up. His eyes were shiny in the dim light of the lantern. He stared at the darkness as though he was searching for something. His unfocused eyes made him look like a mad man.

"Hirate, why did you die?"

Holding his head in both hands, he cried like a child.

"When I drink sake, I become a different person, you know. I couldn't control myself."

Unable to find helpful words, Kicho tentatively rubbed his back.

Unloved by Mother, after losing Father and Hirate, he must feel like an orphan . . . But, I am still here.

The cold wind outside was blowing between tree branches. Kicho felt chilly sitting up on the futon in the night. Slowly, she put her arms around Lord Fool.

He may not have Mother's love, but I want him to know he has my love.

In Kicho's arms, he said,

"I miss Hirate. Little I knew that I relied on him so much . . ."

"Without Hirate's protection, I am helpless." Tears streamed down his cheeks.

"Helpless? No. Seven hundred young men are prepared to die for you. Your brother Katsu may have more retainers, but there is no one who is devoted to him. They are all out for their own gain, using Katsu to their own advantage."

"Is it so?" Lord Fool looked at Kicho without wiping his tears.

"It is so. You've always said that you want men who don't hesitate to risk their lives for you. We all love you."

Kicho watched Lord Fool's profile, as he was calming down, in the soft light of lantern. She felt so much love for him that her heart ached.

"It is my privilege that I alone can be close to you like this, my bare skin next to yours."

Calmed, Lord Fool's fingers slid over Kicho's cheeks, lips and to her breasts.

"I dedicate my life to you," Kicho cried snuggling.

I have fallen in love, against my family in Mino.

Her heart trembled like rippling-waves.

Kicho's long black hair was spread on soft linen. Lord Fool's body draped over her. The air was thick and fragrant with ko[4] incense in the lovers' bedroom. In the soft darkness, the whiteness of his bare bottom rose up and sank. Up then down, it repeated. Outside the bedroom, the sounds of the wind blowing between tree branches was even louder than before. Perhaps a storm was coming. His breathing became urgent.

She extended both her arms onto his muscular hips.

. . . I beg your forgiveness, Father,

Suddenly, from her arms to her spine ran a lightning like sensation. Kicho almost fainted.

*

Kicho received a letter from her father. Lord Viper's powerful yet elegant handwriting said,

"I want to meet my son-in-law Lord Fool. I am tired of hearing everyone say he is a fool. I need to prove them wrong."

Kicho was cautious, remembering her brother Yoshi's message.

Can I really trust Father?

A few days passed. Unlike usual Lord Fool, who would spend all day outside playing mock battles, he enjoyed a leisurely lunch with Kicho. They had bowls of clear soup, char-grilled trout, miso[5] and sesame flavoured stewed bamboo shoots, horse radish salad and steamed rice.

---

4 Type of perfume

5 soybean paste

"Delicious." Kicho wondered what the occasion was.

Putting down his chopsticks, Lord Fool declared,

"I am going to have a cherry blossom viewing party with your father at Shotoku Temple."

Kicho's chopsticks fell on the lacquered table.

"My dear lord. Please re-consider. Shotoku Temple is at the border between Mino and Owari. It is too dangerous for you to go."

Lord Fool watched Kicho's desperate face for a minute and grinned triumphantly.

"Dear Kicho, you have grown to love me more than your father, haven't you?"

Lord Fool rubbed his half-grown beard against Kicho's cheek. Kicho jumped in pain and pleasure at the same time.

Ouch, but, it's good to know he was joking. He is not a fool to be trapped by Father, Viper of Mino.

When she kissed him, his uneven tongue tasted the saltiness of grilled fish.

After lunch, she met with her father's ambassador Hotta and learned that Lord Fool was not joking. The date, the time, the place had been arranged. She felt dizzy.

I am so worried about his safety. It hurts to be in love with a man with no common sense. How can I possibly stop him from going? He just loves to do what is outside of everyone's thinking.

Lord Fool was restless. He woke more than a few times during that night. Every time he woke, he tried to make love and moved frantically. Kicho, however, could not become so passionate. At dawn, Lord Fool went off to survey his territory on his horseback as always. Kicho wiped her tears on the pillow with the faint smell of her lover.

*

In April 1553, Kicho's father and twenty year old Lord Fool met at Shotoku Temple. Nineteen year old Kicho waited at Nagoya Castle knowing the cherry blossom viewing was only an excuse.

Father is trying my husband.

At dusk, Kicho thought she heard horses neigh in the distance. She put her foot into her straw woven zori on a stepping stone to go out to the courtyard, when she heard rhythmical footsteps of the troop approaching. Soon, there was a squeak of the heavy wooden gate. The excited castle gate keeper called,

"Our lord is back."

Kicho wanted to run to the gate, but, she waited. She knew that Lord Fool wouldn't see her until he dismissed the troop. She took a mirror made of shiny silver to powder her face.

She heard familiar footsteps at the end of the long corridor.

He comes to me so soon, today.

Excited, Kicho hurried out to the corridor and sat. There was an unfamiliar figure walking towards her. Showering the glare of the setting sun on his back, the samurai was wearing navy ceremonial hakama trousers and a matching waist coat. The apparel reflected on the shiny floor of the longest corridor of Nagoya Castle. The samurai skilfully kicked the hem of long hakama as he walked regally. Oda crests were shown in white. Wearing a small ceremonial sword and looking distinguished, he had an immaculate samurai hair style . . .

Oh, no . . . Is this my brother-in-law Katsu again?

Eyes firmly fixed on him, Kicho reached her hand between her breast layers of kimono to feel for her dagger.

"My father-in-law is a good man."

A familiar voice called what Kicho wanted to hear the most. Holding her dagger steady, she examined the samurai.

His eyes twinkled, his mouth quivered to form a boyish smile.

"Don't I look handsome?" He beamed at her.

She could not utter a word.

Is he my lord? Is he the man who refused everyone's advice to dress properly? For the very first time in his life, did he get dressed to meet my dear Father?

Cheerful Lord Fool said,

"My father-in-law was kind enough to ride his horse side by side with mine for two kilometres. Ha, ha. He must have felt the need to protect me from his quick thinking retainers. I impressed him with my gun squad and long spear squad. He promised me to send an assisting force in need. We are allies and partners."

"Partners?"

Do you think you are an equal to my father?

Tears ran down Kicho's cheeks as she chuckled.

"I am *so* proud of you."

"Are you crying?"

When he realised that Kicho was overcome with emotions and could not stand up, he squatted down in front of her and took her hands.

"Let's go inside."

The sun had set completely. The maids brought lanterns to light up the peaceful castle.

*

In the following year of 1554, shortly after New Year's Day, Lord Fool was racing his horse to Mino with the icy wind spearing at his cheeks. He was alone. When Lord Fool left his Nagoya Castle at dawn, two of his best horsemen were chasing. Lord Fool's horse, Monokawa, however, was too fast and powerful, the two horsemen were soon left behind.

When Lord Fool arrived at Sagiyama Castle, he knocked on the massive wooden doors at the gate. Sagiyama Castle, situated on the hill near the foot of Mount Kinka, was where Kicho's father spent most of his time in retirement. Monokawa, a large black horse, neighed making white smoke in the wind. Lord Fool wore an appropriate samurai hair style. He looked smart in his pale green kimono, brown riding hakama trousers and a riding coat. As he has given up the Fool's attire, perhaps it is time he should be called Lord Nobunaga by his real name.

Kicho came to greet Lord Nobunaga. She had been there since she came for a New Year's visit, during which time Lord Viper had asked after her love-life and the prospect of his grandson. In a festive white silk kimono with hand painted crimson flowers, she smiled like a blooming flower. She guided Nobunaga through to a smaller lounge filled with the fragrance of fresh pine decoration to mark the New Year.

She thought her husband had come to retrieve her because she had overstayed at her father's palace.

He missed me!

Nobunaga did not smile. "I want to talk privately with Lord Viper."

Kicho twisted her pretty lips and went away.

Lord Viper and his son-in-law had a meeting over a tea ceremony. Kicho and Nobunaga then left the castle. Kicho had tied her hair in a short bundle wearing a man's riding attire. It was far safer not to be spotted as a woman. She asked Nobunaga,

"What was the talk about, my lord?"

"I asked for a favour."

Nobunaga ran his fingers on his beardless chin as he looked at the barren field with the leafless trees of winter. His eyes twinkled blue-grey reflecting the morning sun.

"I'll go ahead. You go home with Toshi.[6]"

Nobunaga strapped Monokawa once. The other horseman, Nagahide followed. He would have no hope of catching up with Nobunaga on Monokawa, but, he belted his horse and lowered his body. The two horses and men became two dots and soon disappeared into the forest.

*

Shincho Koki states that Lord Viper Saito Dosan sent a thousand men to Owari on January 20, 1554. Nobunaga visited Ando, the samurai in charge at the camp and greeted them. The next day, after leaving Ando to guard Nagoya Castle and Kicho, Nobunaga jumped on Monokawa to fight the invaders at the eastern border. The invading Imagawa forces had already built a fort known as Muraki Castle.

Four days later, Nobunaga returned with many dead and injured. A hundred bodiless heads were lined up: Nobunaga "examined" his men's as well as his enemies' heads with due respect. One head after another was brought to him on a wooden board. Many had blood running even after being thoroughly cleaned. He had his secretary document the

[6] 前田利家 Lord Fool's trusted retainer Maeda Toshiie

names of the dead and the names of the men who had struck them down. After an appropriate Buddhist ceremony, the heads and bodies of former enemies and deceased comrades were all buried.

The smell comes into my room in the wind.

Kicho ran to a large pine tree in the courtyard and vomited.

"My lady, you may be with a child," smiled Kano, wiping Kicho's cheek with a cloth. Kicho beamed with saliva running down her chin.

Ando and Kicho had a briefing with one of Ando's men who fought alongside Nobunaga at the fort.

"We had a rain storm on the first night. Lord Nobunaga urged an unwilling skipper to take a boat out into the rough sea to inspect the fort. When he found a castle much better built than he originally believed, the lord started to climb the stone wall himself."

"Himself?" Kicho was dismayed.

"The soldiers had no option but to follow him. They climbed up and fell, climbed only to be speared through. Many were dead or injured. Using all 500 guns, he ordered to keep shooting without interruption. The lord ordered another force to charge into the castle from a weaker point. After a vicious battle we won."

"No wonder so many were dead or injured. Our lord could have been one." Kicho was horrified.

"Lord Nobunaga wept to learn that he lost so many comrades when he returned to the camp."

Ando reported all this to Kicho's father upon returning to Mino. Lord Viper listened to the whole account without blinking even once. "Greeting the troop, urging the skipper, leading the pack, weeping for his men and conducting burials . . ." Lord Viper spat out the words in terror. "My son-in-law has grown to be a ferocious commander."

*

On the night Ando and his men went back to Mino, Kicho said to Nobunaga, "You had taken every single soldier to the battle. You really trusted Ando?"

"Why not?"

"Ando could easily have taken control of Nagoya Castle."

"No way. I left *you,* my wife in charge."

"Did I tell you that Father once told me to stab your back? I am a daughter of the Viper, remember?"

"Don't you dare, my love, ha, ha." Nobunaga pulled Kicho's chin towards him and smiled. He is obviously in a good mood after successfully defending the border.

"You left only me and my maids. If Ando tried, he could easily have seized the castle."

Kicho looked at Nobunaga sternly, but the lantern light was dim and Nobunaga seemed untroubled.

"He would not have, without Father's permission."

"You do trust Father?"

"Yep. He wants his grandson by me."

"Listen, my lord. Did you know that Ando tried to send an envoy to Father to say that there was an opportunity not to be missed . . . to seize the castle."

". . . and you stopped him. Well done, my love!" Nobunaga acted out his surprise, but the way he kept his grin indicated that he had taken Kicho's heroic performance as wife for granted. He must have grown tired of talking. He started to undo the waist string of her satin night robe kimono.

"I have . . ." Kicho was going to say "started my period," but she remembered something much more important.

"I know you took a risk. You were prepared to lose Nagoya Castle and *me*, if I could not guard the castle for you."

"Well . . ." Nobunaga stopped his hands for a moment. "It worked out fine. What on earth are you worried about?"

"If I were not useful, would you abandon me?"

"I know why you are so moody. Having your period? I don't mind." Nobunaga smiled again and pulled Kicho's waist string off.

Kicho remembered that when her mother had a period, her father would go to Miyoshino's bedroom. She was thankful that Nobunaga had so far resisted a concubine, but she needed to ask, "Do you love me?"

"Of course I do. I love your abilities." Nobunaga was sincere.

"It might make sense to you to think that loving and using is the same thing. But, my lord, I am talking about *real* love."

"Real love?" Nobunaga snickered. "You mean the one you read in fairy tales? Grow up, Kicho. You are childish."

"Do you think I am?"

"You are such a baby, Kicho. If you don't want to be dumped, you try harder, don't you? I do. I work my guts out not to be dumped by you."

Kicho giggled. "You are kidding me, my lord."

"Kidding? No way. If I was useless, you would have left me for my brother, Katsu."

"Did you know about *the* scheme? Believe me, my lord. I had no intention of marrying your brother even if you lost your inheritance. This is exactly what I mean by *real* love."

"Losing you probably meant losing my life. Losing me, for you, just meant having Katsu instead. Who do you think would try harder? Which do you think is *real* love?"

Kicho was bemused by Nobunaga's logic.

I know that Father loves me just because I am his daughter. Love between husband and wife, however, may not be so simple. My lord may be right in saying that we both need to work hard to maintain love for each other. I haven't been able to produce a child after five years and Father and my lord are just as anxious as me. Father would have contemplated giving him my younger sister if I was not so head strong. I become depressed every month to see my blood, though my lord has always said, 'wait for another year' to suggestions of a concubine.

Kicho felt chilly in her feet and shoulders. She snuggled to Nobunaga who felt warm like a baby falling asleep. He started to snore, still holding Kicho's waist.

**

"Let us have tea."

When Kicho stood, the whiteness of her leg flashed inside her ankle length Kimono. Shiba's eyes glittered like those of a beast but Nobunaga only glanced at his guest. Twenty year old Kicho wore a green and white Nishijin yarn-dyed kimono without a training hem so she could carry utensils for a tea ceremony. Her long black hair was tied loosely with a matching green woven string at her back. Shiba's eyes followed Kicho until she disappeared to an adjoining room separated by a fusuma.

"Your lady is gorgeous," the middle-aged noble Shiba said to his host. Shiba had, by then, his aristocratic smile.

"I stole the most desirable woman from my brother Katsu. I threatened the Lord of Mino with war until he gave up his beloved daughter."

It was 1554, shortly after the battle of Muraki Castle. Nobunaga had befriended Shiba, who was the Lord of Owari in name only. Shiba lived in Kiyosu, the prosperous capitol of Owari, care of Nobunaga's uncle who held the political powers by his military force.

Kicho brought some treats for the guest. "Please try these. They are from Portugal in Europe."

"They look dainty in either white or pink. They are round and spiky." Shiba picked a piece between his delicate fingers. "Mmm . . . it melts in the mouth. So sweet." Rolling the confectionery on his tongue as he moved his lips, he eyed Kicho.

"They are *Kompeito*," Kicho explained. ". . . made of substance called sugar. Please try these, too. They are made of buckwheat powder and sugar blended together."

"Mmm . . . My son Yoshikane loves sweets."

"Please take some home to him." Nobunaga offered. "By the way, how is my uncle treating you?"

"He does not respect me enough, you know, treating me as his puppet. He enjoys all the powers and extravagant lifestyle as though he were the Lord of Owari."

After this day, Shiba visited Nobunaga often. Nobunaga sometimes made Kicho play "go,"[7] a chess-like game with Shiba. "I am too busy, today."

After Shiba's visits, Nobunaga would without fail sleep at Kicho's chamber. Kicho said one night, "Please don't make me play *go* with Lord Shiba."

"Why not?"

---

[7] It is a board game played by two people using black and white pebbles.

Kicho looked away. Nobunaga pulled her chin. "Tell me."

"When we were alone, Lord Shiba held my hand and . . ."

Nobunaga's lips sealed Kicho's. His faithful servant Juami must have been watching them from behind the fusuma.

A few days later, there was a rumour that Shiba and Nobunaga were conspiring. Nobutomo Oda was so disturbed that after a time of disorder at Kiyosu, he murdered Shiba, whose fourteen year old son escaped to take refuge with Nobunaga.

In the name of young Yoshikane Shiba, who in theory became the Lord of Owari after his father's passing, Nobunaga endorsed the death penalty on Nobutomo, who was guilty of treason. After succeeding with this, Nobunaga patronized young Shiba's return to Kiyosu Castle taking his rightful place as the Lord of Owari. It was apparent then, who suddenly became the most influential man in Owari. Nobunaga, who never took a part in the bloodshed, was only twenty-two.

*

After a meeting with the new Lord of Owari, Nobunaga came back to his lounge, where Kicho sorted his clothes.

"Will you take this hakama to Kiyosu?"

"Of course, it's my favourite . . . At last, we are moving to the capital—but, Imagawa Yoshimoto won't be happy to see me gaining power."

"He is a relation of the Shibas . . . Why not declare your retirement?" Kicho said as she folded Nobunaga's hakama.

"Your father used the trick to curb the rebellion against him, and it worked. Why don't I do the same? I will put young Shiba in the main palace. No one can complain so long as you and I live there as his guardians. We'll live in a house at the back."

"I don't mind to live in a humble house, if it helps you to be safe."

"My uncle kept campaigning for Katsu's succession. If I did not eliminate my uncle first, I would have been his victim."

Kicho realized, then, why Nobunaga befriended the late Shiba in the first place.

My husband is more Viper-like than Father. People were "fooled" by his appearance to call this brain the "Fool". I had no idea that I played a part in Lord Shiba's murder . . .

Her hands trembled as she put Nobunaga's hakama into the bamboo crate.

He'll have the political power in the capital, which is good, but so long as his brother Katsu is around, my husband is not safe. Someone else can revolt again using Katsu . . .

*

Twenty-two year old Kicho was on the way to Nobunaga's lounge after being summoned, in April 1556. Since they came to Kiyosu Castle in the previous year as Shiba's guardians, Nobunaga had gradually extended his residence. A boardwalk leading to Nobunaga's quarter was recently built. The wind blew petals of cherry blossom to the roofed boardwalk. The petals glittered like butterflies in the sun setting in the western side of the castle.

Kicho had recently had heartbreaking news. Her half-brother Yoshi's retainers devised a plot and murdered Kicho's mother and two oldest brothers. Yoshi's retainers had feared that Lord Viper planned to give Yoshi's position as the Lord of Mino to Kicho's full-brother with the Akechi blood line, allowing a monopoly of the political powers by the Akechi clan in Mino. Kicho hurried, fearing whether a battle had started between her distressed father and Brother Yoshi.

It was already dark in the small lounge where Kicho found four boys and two girls facing Nobunaga. The boys looked like trainee priests with freshly shaven heads and black robes. Noticing the girls' delicate feet sticking out of their humble kimono, Kicho wondered who they could be.

Skilfully kicking the training hem of her silk robe, Kicho was about to sit besides Nobunaga on the cushion laid for her on the tatami floor, when the youngest child initiated a sob. Kicho could not believe her eyes.

"Why are you all dressed like this?" Kicho exclaimed. They were Kicho's brothers and sisters. The older boys were Toshiaki, sixteen and Shingoro, fourteen. The smallest girl rushed to Kicho crying.

Nobunaga tried to be cheerful. "Haven't they all grown since I saw them in Mino, two years ago?" He then handed Kicho a letter with a familiar brush hand-writing.

"This is from Father . . . Please send the boys to Myokaku Temple in Kyoto to be priests."

"Isn't it the temple where your grandfather grew up?"

"Father bequests the country of Mino to you? This is a certificate of inheritance for the district of Mino."

Kicho's hands trembled as she scrolled the letter which was in one long piece.

Ignoring Kicho's bewilderment, Nobunaga asked the boys,

"Do you really want to be priests?"

"I want to be a samurai," said Shingoro immediately. The thin sparkling eyes reminded Kicho of her father's eyes.

Will we see Father in our life time again?

Kicho's eyes became moist.

"Will you be my retainer?" Nobunaga asked kindly to Shingoro, who was Kicho's youngest full-brother.

"Please!" Bowing earnestly, Shingoro placed his chubby hands on tatami. Kicho was grateful to Nobunaga's offer and realized that her father's prediction became a reality. Lord Viper had said that his sons would one day tie their horses at Nobunaga's castle. It was unthinkable at the time, because 'to tie one's horse' meant to become a retainer.

*

The air in Kicho's chamber was crisp and fragrant. Nobunaga had embraced Kicho from behind. He remained there still after making love. When Kicho thought he might have gone to sleep, the part of Nobunaga still inside Kicho quivered.

"I'm taking my men to Mino to fight for your father."

Kicho responded with a thankful squeeze, but, she said,

"I appreciate your thought, but, I really don't want you to fight against Brother Yoshi." She wrapped his hand in hers.

"It was Yoshi's retainers who murdered our mother and brothers to fulfil their political ambitions. They had staged Brother Yoshi's fallout from Father to eliminate Akechi's political influence. Brother Yoshi himself must be feeling sorry about the way things turned out."

"Your father has supported me all these years. I can't let him die."

"Most samurai families live at the bottom of the mountain where Yoshi's castle stands at the peak. They have little option but to side with Yoshi. He has seventeen thousand men while Father has only two thousand. It is impossible to win." Kicho held Nobunaga's hand at her breast. "Please do not waste lives to fight an impossible war. Father would not approve of it."

"If I can't win the battle, I will rescue him." Nobunaga felt Kicho's nipples.

She tried to concentrate.

"Father was once a travelling oil merchant with skills in disguising. If he wanted to run for his life, he would have done that long ago. Two thousand men are prepared to die for him, you know. He will not let them down. He must have made up his mind to die in battle. That is why he sent all my remaining brothers and sisters to us."

"Do you think I can be a bystander and watch your father getting murdered? I can't do that to my father-in-law who bequests the land of Mino to me."

Nobunaga divided Kicho's hair at the shoulder and pressed his lips on her neck. When he started to move his hips, she spoke no more.

The next day, a messenger brought the news that the battle between Lord Viper and his son had started. Kicho said to Nobunaga, "My only wish is for your safe return."

Making matters worse for Lord Viper, many of his followers decided to leave him for Yoshi, sensing his imminent victory. By the time Nobunaga led two thousand men to cross the rivers by boats at the Mino-Owari border, Lord Viper had less than a thousand men. Those faithful were prepared to die with him.

*

Nobunaga taking two thousand men meant that the castle was again empty. Without the supporting forces from Lord Viper this time, Kiyosu Castle was vulnerable. Kicho was thankful, nevertheless, that Nobunaga left nineteen year old Juami with her. Although he was a page, a Buddhist servant and not a samurai, his sword skill was above average. His discourteous manners were at times unpopular among other men at the castle, but Kicho liked the way he treated her brothers. Juami treated them as though they were his own younger brothers, rather than his master's relatives.

Kicho climbed up the tower. She was horrified to see a few spot fires in the outskirts of Kiyosu town. She knew that villains within Owari were taking advantage of Nobunaga's absence. She prayed for her husband's return. When it started to get dark, Kicho ordered the maids to light up every corner of the castle to prevent opportunists sneaking in.

With the castle gate squeaking, Kicho heard a long awaited call. "Our lord is back."

My lord is safe, but Father? Kicho sighed in relief and anxiety at the same time.

Before long, Nobunaga's voice approached the courtyard. Accompanying him was Hotta, one of Lord Viper's faithful retainers. Their armour was covered with blood, mud and ashes. They must have travelled through the fires in town, chasing off the invaders. Hotta's face was grey with exhaustion. When he saw Kicho, he crushed down to the ground and pressed his eyelid with the back of his hand. Standing next to Hotta, Nobunaga shook his head from side to side. "I am sorry, Kicho. We were too late."

"Your safe return makes me happy, my lord." Kicho closed her eyes tight trying to stop tears. *Father was killed by his son. An unthinkable tragedy has become reality.*

Kicho's younger brothers and sisters rushed into the room and started to weep. Kicho held the girls in her arms. Shingoro and Juami, who ran into the room a moment later, stopped at the doorway and collapsed on tatami.

"You shall hear the details from Hotta," said Nobunaga and left the courtyard. He would have a mountain of matters to settle before he could come back to his grieving wife.

Hotta took off his helmet blotted with blood and ashes. He hung his head low. The balding head had tangled fibres of black and white hair. Kneeling on the ground, he wiped his eye again with the back of his hand. "It was Komaki, he who struck my lord."

"Komaki?" Kicho could not believe. "Komaki was Father's retainer. He was a page. I feel for Father's anguish." Kicho bit her lips.

Hotta said, "Lord Viper observed the way Lord Yoshi conducted the battle. He said, 'I am proud of my son. Mino shall be peaceful for some years to come.' He then went out to the foremost line of the battle on the gravelled surface of the River. He was suicidal. Lord Yoshi's men tried to capture my lord alive, when Komaki came out of nowhere and struck him down."

Kicho felt a tear go down her cheek.

I knew he loved Brother Yoshi. I don't believe Yoshi wanted to kill our father.

Hotta cried, "I wanted to die with my lord. But he said to me, 'You must go and let my death be known to Nobunaga immediately. Today is not the day for him to fight, endangering precious lives for no gain. Nobunaga is a man who can bring peace and order to Japan, one day. You shall live and work for him.'" Hotta scrunched his double layered eye lids.

Kicho climbed down the stone steps to hold Hotta's hand.

Father, who was once mighty Lord Viper of Mino, had decided to die early to save the lives of others . . .

Kicho's courtyard was lit brightly by bonfires. A sudden gust of wind brought a petal of cherry blossom onto Kicho's long black hair.

*

On the 18th day of July 1556, the year that Kicho's father passed away in April, Kicho and Nobunaga were honoured guests at a house warming party at Hotta's new residence in Tsushima. Hotta's family were generations of celebrants at Tsushima Shrine.

"I hear that you are a good dancer, my lord," said Hotta with a grin.

"Sure. Let's have fun."

Nobunaga's men were already merry after having *sake.* They danced dressed as red and black demons. Nobunaga, who didn't need sake to be jolly, was a fairy.[8] Everyone danced and laughed until there were tears in their eyes. Nobunaga said,

"Because I kidnapped Kicho on the way to the main castle, we've only had a simple wedding at Nagoya Castle. I have been too busy with battles since, to have a proper reception. Kicho wants me to hold a function to honour her at Kiyosu, the capital of Owari. Can you all come?"

"With our pleasure, Lord Nobunaga."

The elders at Tsushima nodded.

"I will pronounce that I have inherited Mino from my father-in-law."

"We are all longing for your son, my lord," said Hotta.

Nobunaga looked around for Kicho. She was getting changed in another room to go out to the festival.

"Do not mention it in front of Kicho. She is depressed about our childlessness."

"How about taking a concubine, Lord Nobunaga?"

"Concubine? No. She'd be jealous and not worth it. I am the Fool, you know. I never know when I die. If I die, Brother Katsu and his son shall take over."

Hotta looked around and said quietly. "My lord, that is exactly what I am worried about. Having a son would curb the assassination attempts that you have had recently."

Nobunaga was silent for a moment. He then said, "Do you think so?"

"Of course, my lord. Please, take a concubine and have your son adopted by Lady Kicho. Your son will be the rightful lord of Owari as well as Mino, one day. I'll talk to our lady. I am sure she will understand.

---

[8] Shincho Koki

It is absurd for a lord of your status not to have a concubine after seven long years of childless marriage."

Leaving Hotta's residence together, Kicho and Nobunaga went to the Tsushima Shrine annual festival. Having only a few bodyguards, twenty-two year old Kicho and her twenty-three year old husband were dressed simply as villagers of Owari. After a hot and humid day, Kicho relished the fresh breeze by the river. She snuggled Nobunaga on a cosy makeshift viewing platform to watch the reflection of the numerous lights on the straw boats cruising peacefully down the river. He was kind. Trusting her husband's eternal love, like other women in Owari, it was a romantic memory that Kicho treasured for many years.

*

Several weeks later, on a hot day after a typhoon in August 1556, cicadas were deafening in the trees of Kiyosu Castle.

"My lord, my lord," Sakuma ran to Nobunaga, spitting saliva out from a gap of his missing tooth. "Your brother Katsu's retainers are reaping rice from our lady's paddy field without permission."

Kicho had a private property that she managed directly, on the other side of Kiyosu Castle, but it was too early in the season to reap the rice. Nobunaga ordered Sakuma to build a fortress in the area and defend the property until he gathered his forces. Unfortunately, it rained and poured on the 23rd August to rupture the bridge. The next day, assuming that Nobunaga's forces could not cross the river, Katsu's men started to demolish Sakuma's makeshift fortress. Sakuma had only three hundred men to defend it with, against seventeen hundred soldiers of Katsu. After a furious defence with stones and arrows, Sakuma's men exhausted all their weapons. They had no option but to concede.

A scream thundered behind the hill.

"Traitors!"

Nobunaga on Monakawa's back galloped leading seven hundred men. Nobunaga's eyes were fired up. Katsu's men, ill prepared for the sudden attack, were thunderstruck. Nobunaga had surveyed various parts of the river by running Monokawa in and out, backwards and forwards until he found a shallow enough spot for all his men including his foot soldiers to cross.

Katsu's force, however, had twice as many men. After a violent clash, many were injured and retreated. Before long, only twenty men were left guarding Nobunaga, who himself had several cuts and wounds from sword fights.

Hayashi, Katsu's best swordsman and Kuroda, one of Nobunaga's samurai fought against each other for a long time. They were both exhausted and panting. They kept eyeing at each other, seeking the chance for a final blow. Gathering all his remaining strength, Hayashi threw his sword down at Kuroda who defended himself with his sword. As Kuroda screamed in pain, his left hand fell on the muddy paddy field. Nobunaga saw this and struck Hayashi from behind. Hayashi fell.

"You traitor!" Nobunaga swung his long sword down at Hayashi, who was struggling to get up. When Nobunaga's sword swayed again, Hayashi's head flew up into the air with a sound of blood spurting from his neck. The bodiless head landed in the mud two metres away, making a dull splatter sound. Hayashi's eyes stared at the sky, his mouth curving still in agony. His white head band he wore around his untied hair was coated with blood and mud.

Shibata, Katsu's chief samurai ran back to his master, who was waiting for a victorious news. Shibata was dangling a piece of blood-spattered cloth around his neck to nurse his injured arm. His face was grey and his clothes were encrusted in blood and mud.

Katsu was shocked. "We had twice as many men. How could we lose?"

"We never expected Lord Nobunaga cross the flooded river. Our men were terrified by Lord Nobunaga's scream. I tried in vain to stop them from running away. Hayashi's men were the same once he was struck down."

"What? Hayashi got struck down?"

"I am sorry, my lord. It is hard to believe that Lord Nobunaga's forces made of peasant boys could defeat our army of samurai."

Nobunaga had met more than a few consecutive assassination attempts and rebellions straight after Kicho's father's death. This famous coup attempt by Katsu's retainers, initiated by rooting Kicho's private property, also, was only four months after Lord Viper's death. If he had not had Kicho's love and Lord Viper's support, Lord Fool might not have survived to his adulthood.

*

In October, 1556, Akechi Castle fell to the Lord of Mino, Kicho's half-brother Yoshi. Kicho's cousin Hide and his wife narrowly escaped, assisted by Nobunaga's cousin, who unfortunately died in the violent battle. Kicho felt sorry for this man's widow, Kitsuno, who was also Nobunaga's cousin and employed her as a maid at the castle. Kitsuno will later become an important woman in Kicho's life. Nobunaga also offered an employment to Hide, who declined for a reason that only Kicho could guess. Hide went away to explore various parts of Japan for several years seeking work.

*

About a year later, in early October, 1557, Kicho thought she heard a clatter from the castle gate. Nobunaga on Monokawa's back jumped a low bamboo fence into the courtyard. He then hopped onto the tatami lounge without taking off his footwear. Staggering behind him was a young page with a large medical box.

"Your back is soaked," Kicho gasped, ". . . in blood!"

"I pulled an arrow out myself. Monokawa panicked when he got one in his bottom and I nearly fell off."

"Was it Hayashi again?"

"Hayashi's been trying to revenge his brother, younger Hayashi, whom I struck down last year."

"If you don't do something, you won't see the New Year's Day."

Kicho tended his wound. Nobunaga stopped going outside for a few weeks, and Kicho went to Suemori castle to say he was gravely ill from the infected wound and that Katsu should apoligize for not controlling Hayashi. Lady Dota urged Katsu to make amends before Nobunaga's passing.

On the second day of November 1557, Nobunaga had just finished breakfast in Kicho's lounge when he heard,

"Lord Katsu and Hayashi are here to see you."

Nobunaga's eyes glittered. He called two of the best swordsmen in his household and briefed them in the corridor. When Nobunaga returned to Kicho, there was a flame burning in his eyes. Kicho shivered remembering what had happened when her mother and brothers visited "sick" Brother Yoshi.

Shortly afterwards, the two men returned and kneeled on the floor of the corridor. Kicho turned to see splashes of fresh blood on their white kimonos.

"Lord Katsu honourably committed seppuku, obeying your orders."

Kicho let her shoulders down. Nobunaga closed his eyes.

The swordsmen sat on the wooden corridor hanging their heads.

The amount of blood tells me that there was a struggle rather than "obeying" orders. It must be obvious to my lord also. His face is grey and it is not because he has not been outside for a month. It reminds me of the dead soldiers he brings back after a battle.

She closed her eyes.

Nobunaga staggered out of the room. Kicho put her fingers together on tatami and bowed to her husband. The back of his shoulders looked as thin as a real sick person. Kicho waited till he was out in the corridor before she let out a sigh.

He is going to inspect his brother's body . . . to confirm that Owari is now a safer place for him.

*

"How did Mother take it?"

"She shed a few quiet tears," said Kicho.

"You are lying?"

"I am sorry."

Nobunaga had sent Kicho to Suemori Castle to report the incident to Lady Dota, who was outraged.

"Katsu was always her favourite boy. When he was born, Mother was happy to send me to Nagoya Castle with Hirate."

"I explained that Hayashi rebelled in the name of Katsu . . ."

"She said it was not Katsu's fault, right?"

"You did the right thing, my lord. While Lord Katsu was alive, another retainer would use him to revolt, again and again."

"You made me kill my brother." He put his palm on his forehead and turned his back.

"It was necessary to stop further assassination attempts. You had forgiven Katsu twice, because Mother begged you to. You can't afford to have any more rebellions."

Kicho tried to hug him from behind, but he shrugged her hands off.

"Mother will hate me now," he groaned.

"I am sorry, my lord." Nobunaga was silent.

"Why did you spare Hayashi?" asked Kicho.

"I need him."

"He conspired against you three times. Don't you hate him?"

"Hate? He is capable and respected. If I don't make peace with him, I have to have a battle with him. Well, maybe, that's what I really want, but, I can't." Nobunaga snickered. "Not, now."

Kicho wondered what he might do later. It will take her twenty-three years to find out.

*

Kicho woke in the middle of the night and walked towards the wash room. In the courtyard outside a spare room, she noticed a slight monkey-faced man squatting.

"Cheeky devil. Are you trying to sneak into my maid's bedroom?"

"I beg your mercy, my lady."

Who would bother to share a night with this ugly man? My maids are all attractive and well-bred. If a maid gets pregnant I either have her married or send her home. Either way, I would dismiss her: There cannot be anyone who would sleep around . . .

On the way *back,* Kicho sensed that there was someone hiding. She ordered a maid light up the corner of a bush.

"I know it is you, Monkey.[9] Come here, right now."

"My lady . . ."

"Show me what you are hiding in your chest pocket."

Monkey hesitated at first, but eventually put his hand between his kimono layers. When she saw it, Kicho's face turned blue under the moonlight. It was a pair of zori footwear with familiar green bands.

The owner of the zori is in the room with a maid of mine, having Monkey wait outside.

Kicho wanted to scream. Instead, she held her breath and pronounced,

"Thank you, Monkey."

She staggered back to her chamber which was only a small bedroom; because Kicho and Nobunaga lived in a modest house within the property of the castle as guardians for the young lord. It was late autumn; there were only a few surviving crickets calling infrequently for mates in the courtyard. Not a sound came from the small room next to the kitchenette; but Kicho noticed the faintest light within and even a hint of Ko perfume in the air.

He was listening to me in the arms of my maid.

Kicho felt her blood boil. She returned to her futon and cried under the doona. She was too proud to let anyone know that she was upset. She remembered her late mother's wisdom to be kind to concubines and to hide jealousy. She felt miserable that she could not follow it.

It was easy for Mother. She had five children. It is harder for me because I am barren.

Kicho sobbed all night. The next morning, she looked at herself in the polished silver mirror with subtle bellflower patterns at the back. It was the engagement present from Hide.

---

9 Nobunaga nicknamed him "saru" meaning monkey. He would later call himself Hideyoshi Toyotomi, one of the most famous men in Japanese history.

I have red eyes! The hateful mirror reflects them too clearly. How embarrassing. It is all Hide's fault. I have to endure this torment because he didn't marry me . . .

She hurled the mirror onto the tatami. The mirror bounced back with a thud.

Kicho wondered who the offensive woman could be. Kicho's young maids were all frightened of Nobunaga because of his boisterous way. Four years senior to Kicho, Kano was an exception. She would engage in a conversation with Nobunaga at ease. Nobunaga willingly gave her leave to go home to Mino, and he would eagerly listen to her when she returned, to gather military information. Kicho did not want to believe that her trusted chief maid betrayed her, but she was too afraid to ask. She feared that if she lost her temper in the process, faithful Kano might commit suicide to pay for her "crime".

Though she is my entrusted maid, Kano is also a woman. If she had made a mistake, I don't want to lose her.

Kicho was depressed with the thought of having to endure her fate that her best friend had slept with her husband.

A few days later, Kicho remembered that there was another woman not scared of Nobunaga. *It cannot be. She is too old and ugly.*

Seven years senior to Kicho, twenty-nine year old Kitsuno was Nobunaga's cousin and the widow of a man who died in the battle at Akechi Castle.

After having Kitsuno, Nobunaga became as blissful as the time before Katsu's assassination attempts. Kicho knew that she should celebrate her husband's well-being, but it wasn't easy. On some nights, Nobunaga's naturally high-pitched voice or laughter travelled from *the* room.

His hands, his lips, his tongue and . . .

She tried in vain not to imagine their legs entwining.

I would tolerate it if she was young and pretty, but how can I approve an ugly old woman stealing my young husband? She looks like her aunt, my mother-in-law . . . Did he want her love to make up for his mother's love? Did he want her slender body similar to his mother's? Would he suck her breasts? Did she miss having a man so soon after her husband's passing?

What a bitch she is . . . I should punish her by dragging her around by her long black hair, or perhaps she would better deserve to be speared through . . .

Kicho, however, was at times regretful.

Who would know Nobunaga's barren wife can be so selfishly jealous? Shame on me.

When Nobunaga visited Kicho, he came through the public corridor. When he came to *that* horrid woman, however, he would come discreetly from the courtyard. Kicho learned the agony of unwittingly listening to the slightest sound in the courtyard on a quiet night. One night, she heard *that* sound. The sound of Nobunaga's zori footsteps stopped outside of *that* room. After a short time, Kicho heard his voice outside of *that* room.

Leaving so soon?

She held her breath. Kano's calm voice announced,

"The lord is here to see you, my lady."

"How rude could he be to visit his wife after finishing with a concubine?"

To her surprise, however, she was cheerfully combing her hair and patting her satin night robe. She was thrilled that he is coming to her.

Nobunaga came in and sat solemnly.

"I think I should give Kitsuno her own room."

"Her own room?" Kicho scantily thought of her late mother's words, "be kind to your concubines," but it was too late. She had lost control.

"Why don't you give her *my* room, and let me go back to Mino."

"Don't be jealous, Kicho. Out of a dozen warlords in Japan, only Mohri and I don't have any concubines. Mohri's wife had three sons and a daughter. You've been barren for eight long years. Don't you understand that we need a son, an heir? Grow up and endure, Kicho. Which part of Mino are you going back to anyway? Akechi Castle fell and Hide is unemployed."

"I am going back to Brother Yoshi."

"Don't be silly. He is your foe who killed your parents and brothers."

"I believe he had no intention of killing my parents or brothers. I know he regrets what has happened. He would be happy to have me back before you start a full scale battle with him. It is customary to return a hostage before the war."

"Have I ever treated you as a hostage?" Nobunaga grew red and shook his fist.

When Kicho saw his eyes well, she was sorry.

"I am barren . . ." Her lips quivered and tears fell. She was sorry for herself.

Nobunaga hugged her satin clad shoulders.

"Don't cry, Kicho."

His kindness made her more upset. She nodded and cried like a child.

"You want a baby, right? It's really easy to have a baby, didn't you know?" Nobunaga said caringly, "You shall adopt Kitsuno's baby."

"What?" Kicho exclaimed. "Is she pregnant? Already?"

How can I forgive a woman who falls pregnant?

Devastated, Kicho looked up at her husband. She was pale, but, he didn't seem to notice it in dimly lit room. Because she stopped crying, he became cheerful.

"Your adopted son shall be the future Lord of Owari and Mino, as I inherited Mino from your father."

"My son will be your successor . . . ?" Kicho managed to wipe her tears at last, but not without endeavor.

"If I die prematurely, I want you to have a secure status in the Oda household as the mother of the successor. So, don't you ever say that you are going back to Mino, again, Promise?" Nobunaga saw Kicho nod and happily added,

"Oh, Kitsuno doesn't need a room. She can have the baby at her brother's place."

"Do you mean to send Kitsuno back to her family? Really?"

Kicho could not believe her husband's kind consideration.

I don't have to listen to the dreaded footsteps again!

"I forgot that I was not the lord of the castle. I am merely the guardian for Shiba. Well done, Kicho, to remind me of that. I am allowed only one consort; that is you."

Well, he has other reasons, but no matter. I am the only wife.

". . . You know, Kicho. Father died prematurely at forty-two, because he indulged in sake and teenage concubines. I've given up sake since Hirate's death, you know, and I chose Kitsuno because she was old and ug . . ."

"You liar!"

Kicho slapped Nobunaga, but her wet eyes managed a smile.

I know that he has become radiant. He is in love, I know, but no matter. He loves me more.

"Young virgins have the right to fall in love and get married like you. I just wanted a baby, so I chose Kitsuno, who would know her place as a concubine and your humble servant . . ."

Kicho chuckled. "Let's not talk about Kitsuno, any more. Don't worry, my lord. I am sorry that I was childish."

"I will stay with you tonight."

Kicho wanted to express her love and gratitude for Nobunaga in many ways. Resting in his muscular arms, she thought of her late father.

Father loved me till the day he died, even though I could not give him a grandson, Nobunaga's heir that he wanted so much. His gift of Mino to Nobunaga protects the happiness of my siblings and I, long after Father's passing. I shall dedicate my life to my husband who takes care of Father's legacy to unite Japan to end the civil war.

Kicho remembered her father's words, "The weaker should obey the mightier as quickly as possible to unify Japan before too many young men die."

*

Kicho heard Nobunaga's voice from an unlikely place. When she went into the kitchen, Juami was kowtowing flat on the cold clay floor.

"If I catch you again, I will slash your head off," said Nobunaga and off he went.

"What on earth was he upset about?"

Kicho wanted to know, but, Juami looked away.

"It does not matter, my lady. It was my fault."

Kicho noticed a tear on his eyelash.

A kitchen maid said to Kicho,

"Juami was unlucky, my lady. The lord happened to see him fondling Nene."

"I wonder why the lord came to the kitchen. Toshi must have said something to the lord."

The next day, Toshi chased Juami.

"Give it back!"

"Catch me if you can."

Slender Juami went through a gap in the hedge, but big Toshi couldn't and he marched on the spot fuming. Toshi recently got engaged and the ornamental sword grip, which he showed off to everyone, was a present from his fiancée. Nobunaga was watching with a grin, but he intervened when he saw Toshi pulling out a sword from its case.

"Can't you see Juami teases you because you take everything too seriously?"

Toshi put his sword back in the case, but he kept eying Juami.

"Expect my revenge."

Kicho was worried.

They grew up competing for the lord's love. Toshi will be married soon, but Juami, a priest, is not allowed a wife. I should ask Toshi to be more tactful with Juami.

Before Kicho had a chance to talk to Toshi, he and Juami were involved in another fight and, in unfortunate circumstances, Juami was fatally wounded. Kicho, fearing Nobunaga's punishment on Toshi, opened the back gate and he escaped from the castle. Kicho went back to lifeless Juami and wept.

*

Within three years, Nobunaga had four children—two sons and a daughter by Kitsuno, and a third son by another concubine. By January 1559, Lord Nobunaga had united all Owari. He employed farmers' second and third sons to construct roads, river banks and bridges. He trained them as foot soldiers. The farmers were no longer forced to abondon farm work to fight in the war and there were no more villains or highway robbers. Residents were happy with Lord Nobunaga and he gradually extended his eastern border to widen his territory.

Yoshimoto Imagawa, the head of the powerful neighbouring clan to the east was related to Shiba. They were not happy with Nobunaga acting like the lord of Owari. The young lord Shiba conspired to murder Nobunaga upon Yoshimoto's instructions. Nobunaga found out about the plan through his Ninja and chased Shiba away to Kyoto. Yoshimoto was furious and decided to invade Owari to crush Nobunaga by military force. Yoshimoto was determined not to make a mistake. His force had as many as fifty thousand men; ten times Nobunaga's. In such a circumstance, the weaker would of course submit without a fight. Nobunaga's retainers had expected the same and Nobunaga had not denied this option.

On the eve of Yoshimoto's imminent attack, Nobunaga called the Sakuma brothers, who had been given important forts to guard near the border, to Kiyosu Castle. They arrived knotting their eyebrows.

Nobunaga said tentatively,

"Why don't you stay here at Kiyosu tonight?"

"No way, my lord,"

Younger Sakuma groaned spitting saliva out from the gap of his missing tooth.

"Four hundred faithful men and I will guard the fort to our end."

Nobunaga looked away biting his lips. He walked the Sakuma brothers to the castle gate and embraced them one after another.

"Wait for me in another world."

The glaring sun was about to set but it was still hot and humid. The Sakuma brothers mounted their horses. Two horses walked side by side as their masters lamented. "Even Lord Nobunaga's wisdom mirror is fogged up this time. He has no vision."

Nobunaga went to bed early. The evening passed. When it was still dark, on 19th May, 1560, Nobunaga's page Sawaki screamed as he ran to the chamber.

"The attack, my lord, the attack! They are attacking the forts at the border."

Nobunaga said to Kicho,

"A hand drum."

He stood in the middle of her private lounge and opened his dancing fan. He sang and danced to Kicho's hand drum.

"A man's life of fifty years under the sky is nothing compared to the age of this world. Life is but a fleeting dream, an illusion—Is there anything that lasts forever?" It was Nobunaga's favourite verse from Atsumori.

This may be the last time we perform together. His voice is so serene.

Nobunaga danced twice and closed his fan. It was hot and humid. Kicho perspired while helping Nobunaga put on the armour. Nobunaga had three bowls of rice porridge standing up. "I won't need lunch, if I live till afternoon."

Nobunaga looked larger than life in his armour. His eyes sparked with fighting spirit.

"I'll leave you in charge, Kicho. I'll take all the men. We can't ask your father for help anymore."

"Never be concerned about us, my lord," said Kicho. She concealed her fear of death.

Nobunaga's eye lids were pink. "We are off." He left Kicho.

The eastern sky was faintly purple. Following Nobunaga on Monokawa's back, were Sawaki and four others. The other retainers, who knew nothing about Nobunaga's plan, jumped up and chased the master: Within ten minutes, the castle was empty except for a handful of women. Nobunaga and his followers went to Atsuta Shrine but Kicho did not even know that.

Two year old Kicho's adopted daughter, Toku crawled towards her. Nobunaga's two younger sons played sumo wrestling in the courtyard and Toku wanted to see them. She got dangerously close to the edge of the veranda, when her babysitter picked her up just in time.

She can crawl so fast now. Innocent children have no idea about the crisis we are in. Kicho managed to smile at Nobunaga's heir, Lord Strange, when her eyes met with his. Nobunaga had nicknamed him after the way he felt to meet his first born. Lord Strange was wearing a miniture suit of armour, complete with an ornate helmet fit for a commander—It was a recent gift from Nobunaga.

He is so proud.

Kicho smiled again.

It was Lord Strange's turn to wrestle. Four-year-old Lord Strange was pushed by his quick younger brother, Lord Three-seven, and lost his balance; obviously Lord Strange's heavy armour was his handicap.

"Take it off," said three-year-old Lord Three-seven.

"No. Let's wrestle again. I won't be beaten this time, Three-seven," said Lord Strange getting up. Lord Three-seven was Nobunaga's third son by another concubine although he was actually a few weeks older than "the second" son by Kitsuno.

Kicho smiled at Lord Strange. Kicho's eighteen year old brother Shingoro watched him.

Since Juami's death, they became closer. I am responsible for these children's lives. If my lord does not come home tonight, they must flee the castle in plain clothes. It is safer for them to go in four different directions. I'll get Shingoro to take Lord Strange, my adopted son and Nobunaga's heir. I miss Juami who used to give me so much support when our lord was away. I wonder where Toshi is. He fled the castle after killing Juami and my lord has gone to the most dangerous battle of his life without his best body guard . . .

It was nearly noon. Under the blazing sun, injured soldiers kept arriving—several of them at a time.

"Oh, no! The fort has fallen, already? Sakuma dead?" Kicho remembered Sakuma's missing front tooth and put her hands together in prayers. Sakuma's fort was attacked and taken by Yasu, [10] (whose infant name was Takechiyo) who had been a six-year-old surety in Owari when Kicho was newly wed. Nobunaga used to take him riding and swimming in the river. After two years in Owari with Nobunaga, Yasu was sent to Yoshimoto through a surety exchange treaty. He lived within Yoshimoto Imagawa's household and had since married to a niece of Yoshimoto. Leaving his wife and baby daughter behind in the care of Yoshimoto's household, Yasu was forced to obey Yoshimoto's orders and fight against Nobunaga.

Every time the castle gate made an eerie noise, Kicho knew that there were more injured men at the gate. The gate keeper made sure that they were allies before opening the gate, but he would have to face invaders for a fatal fight before long. The sun had risen high up in the

---

[10] Tokugawa Ie(yasu)

blue sky without a cloud. It was a hot day. The castle hall was filled with the smell of the blood and sweat of men. Kicho disinfected their wounds with pure *sake* alcohol. Men screamed in pain. Kicho got them to bite a piece of cloth so they wouldn't damage their teeth by clenching them too tight.

When the invaders arrive, these men will keep them at bay while I let the children escape.

Kicho prayed for Nobunaga's return. She knew what her husband went out for and that he wouldn't return alive unless he achieved it—getting Yoshimoto's head. It seemed almost impossible: A win against a force ten times as large?

Kicho climbed up the tower of the castle. She was horrified to see spot fires around the outskirts of Kiyosu.

The invaders have arrived and started burning crops and farm houses. On a hot windy day like this, the fire will quickly spread.

Bearing shaky knees, Kicho climbed down the narrow steps one at a time.

I am not telling this to the maids. There is no point in making them panic.

She sneaked into the Buddhist prayer room and prayed for rain. Before long, black clouds appeared in the western sky rapidly spreading eastwards and covering the entire sky. Huge drops of rain started to fall.

Thank God. Kiyosu town is saved from an inferno—for a time. When the main invading forces arrive, we have no way to survive. There's nowhere to hide in this vast plain from the search of the invaders.

*

Nobunaga had gathered his soldiers at Zensho temple. Among official Oda banners, upon closer look, there were many obscure makeshift banners made by nearby farmers who wanted to help Nobunaga. Leaving the banners behind to make his enemies believe his main force was still at Zensho temple, Nobunaga led his army detouring along secondary pathways. He planned to get as close as possible to Yoshimoto without him knowing for a surprise attack. On the way, he heard that the younger Sakuma had died and the forts had fallen. Black cloud covered the sky and large drops of rain started to fall.

"Your 500 guns are wet and useless, my lord. It is hopeless. Let's retreat." begged Hayashi holding Monakawa's reign.

"No. Today is the day that one of us will die, either Yoshimoto or I. I will proceed, Sakuma, your death will not be wasted." Nobunaga took out a string of beads for Buddhist prayer. Soon, he heard the first good news of the day.

"Lord Yoshimoto has stopped for lunch at Okehazama valley."

"Really?" Nobunaga smiled for the first time that day.

"Yoshimoto may have 50,000 men, but they are stretched out thinly along the highway. We will attack the unsuspecting Yoshimoto and strike him down before his other forces arrive."

Nobunaga and 4,000 men progressed in rain, along the pathways of Owari known only to locals. Nobunaga had a glimpse of the front line of the enemy force marching towards Kiyosu. He detoured to reach the top of the cliff of Okehazama valley. The rain had stopped and the mist started to clear. What Nobunaga saw was too good to be true.

"I've won," he declared.

He saw Yoshimoto's quarters at the bottom of the cliff. From an unmistakable marquee with the crest of two white lines on black, came a faint sound of hand drums and singing. Yoshimoto must be relaxing or even celebrating a premature win. His troop rested under the trees, in the scant shade they could find. Many had taken their armour off to cool down. The armour they had been wearing under the scorching sun must have become unbearably hot—Nobunaga could almost see the steam coming out of shiny armour drenched in rain.

"The only target is Yoshimoto—Yoshimoto alone," shouted Nobunaga.

"Sir."

"Run through the foot soldiers. Don't bother with individual samurai or prize heads. When we win, the honour will belong to all that participated in this historic battle. Generations of our descendants will be proud of us."

"Sir."

"You only die once, never twice. Die for me!"

"Sir."

When Yoshimoto heard the noise, he thought it was a gang of highway robbers; the bannerless troop had no identification. Soon, Yoshimoto realized that he was in a serious battle. Nobunaga lead the warriors directly to Yoshimoto's marquee to meet three hundred swordsmen standing between him and the marquee. Many had no time to put their armour back on. Twice, three times, Nobunaga and his men attacked the sea of swordsmen. Four times, five times. Many fell. Many ran away. There was a wall of fifty ferocious men. The fire in their eyes showed that they were prepared to die for Yoshimoto.

"Go and kill the Fool of Owari!" Yoshimoto yelled at his warriors inside the marquee. "Go and get him. Big prize on his head. Kill him. Go!"

Yoshimoto's skilled warriors come out of marquee targeting Nobunaga on Monokawa's back. One throws a spear at Nobunaga. Nobunaga ducks behind Monokawa's head. Monokawa, speared through the neck, falls. No time for a spare horse. Nobunaga makes his way to the marquee, slashing at the foot soldiers swarming at him.

"Yoshimoto is in the marquee," Nobunaga yelled.

"Don't let him escape. Go around from the other side. Get Yoshimoto. Strike him and die with him."

Nobunaga's warrior, a small and quick man named Koheita, went under, through the forest of fighting men. He ran around to reach the marquee from the other side. Yoshimoto was alone inside with a Buddhist monk, shaking prayer beads. Koheita speared Yoshimoto in his side.

Yoshimoto groaned. He swung his long sword and cut Koheita's leg in half at the knee.

Koheita screamed. He hopped swinging his sword in the air.

Yoshimoto, holding his long sword, aimed at Koheita's throat. Another of Nobunaga warriors, Shinsuke pushed past Koheita. Shinsuke and Yoshimoto fell together. Shinsuke climbed on top of Yoshimoto and bashed his face. Yoshimoto opened his mouth, showing his blackened teeth and bit Shinsuke's hand. Bearing the pain in the finger, Shinsuke pinned Yoshimoto's head down to the ground. Shinsuke's free left hand rose up high, aiming to stab at Yoshimoto's throat with the tip of his long sword. He missed, nearly cutting his own wrist. He lifted his left arm again. Blood spewed out of Yoshimoto's throat, but Yoshimoto did not let go of Shinsuke's little finger. Shinsuke stabbed again. When his hand was free, Shinsuke grabbed Yoshimoto's hair and severed the neck bone.

"I got him," Shinsuke stood, grasping Yoshimoto's long hair. He tossed the head in the air. Blood splattered out of Yoshimoto's neck to Shinsuke's face.

"I got him,"

Shinsuke wiped tears smearing blood over his face. His little finger rolled out of Yoshimoto's mouth and fell on the bloody grass of Okehazama valley.

*

Three days after the battle of Okehazama, Nobunaga rode a horse into Mino, accompanied by Mori and Shingoro. Nobunaga rode a brown horse as Monokawa had died at Okehazama. The following day, Nobunaga held a conference with Kicho and senior retainers at the largest hall of Kiyosu Castle.

"Congratulations to us all for striking down Lord Imagawa Yoshimoto," said he.

"The first person to take my sake cup is the man who informed me that Yoshimoto stopped for lunch at Okehazama. He will also get a piece of land as a reward. The second honour goes to Koheita who first speared Yoshimoto. The third honour belongs to Shinsuke who struck Yoshimoto down to take his head."

The men looked at each other.

"Well, my lord, doesn't the first prize go to the man who struck him down?" Hayashi said.

"The victory belongs to us all in the Oda household. I had told you right at the beginning not to worry about prize heads."

Shinsuke with his missing little finger nodded happily, so no one was going to dispute Nobunaga.

"Today, a kind person has given me lots of abalones to share with you," said Nobunaga.

"Mmm—Abalones," Shibata licked his lips.

"Who gave us such expensive gifts, my lord?" said Hayashi.

"There are dried abalones for you to take home to your family, as well." Nobunaga said.

"Who would be so generous?" They looked at each other.

Nobunaga laughed with his mouth wide open.

"They think you are tight fisted, Kicho."

Twenty-six year old Kicho smiled. Wearing an elaborate gown, she looked like a blooming flower.

"It was our lady?" Shinsuke nursed his finger that Kicho had bandaged.

"Kicho *cut* the abalones in strips, *beat* them flat, and dried them." Everyone at the hall knew that "cut" and "beat" were auspicious words relating to war victory.

"Our lady herself . . . ?" The retainers looked at Kicho as though she was the moon-goddess.

"Matsu will weep in appreciation," Toshi whispered about his young wife. He curled his wide shoulders behind Monkey's small body. Kicho had invited Toshi to come to the celebration hoping Nobunaga would forgive him and take him back at the castle. Nobunaga glanced at Toshi, and said nothing. Nobunaga had not seen Toshi since he fled eighteen months ago. He must have noted the three prize heads presented by Toshi at the inspection ceremony. Kicho saw Toshi looking away almost crying. There was no kind word given to him by Nobunaga. Not a smile, not even a nod.

Nobunaga looked around. "Does anyone know why Kicho is giving you abalones?"

"It must be to celebrate the victory," said Sakuma. He did not talk about his younger brother who died guarding the fort.

"I don't think that is it," said Nobunaga.

"Well, then, my lady?" Shibata gave up.

"It is to show my gratitude," said Kicho, "for deciding to avenge my father's enemy in Mino." She bowed to her retainers.

The retainers looked at each other dumbfounded. Who had thought of invading Mino—the most powerful neighbouring district? Didn't we just win an unwinnable battle? Shouldn't we be satisfied?

A loud voice came from a small man right at the end of the hierarchy.

"We thank you for your kindness, our lady. Of course, we all have sincere wishes to attack your enemy in Mino," declared Monkey.

Nobunaga nodded at Monkey. He employed many Mino samurai who had mixed feelings for attacking Kicho's half-brother, Yoshi. It was very important for them to have Kicho showing a clear direction regarding Yoshi, that he was their common enemy who struck down Kicho's father, Lord Viper. Kicho understood that she must choose between Brother Yoshi or Nobunaga as Yoshi repeatedly tried to kill Nobunaga. She finally made up her mind to call her brother an enemy to avenge her father. There was a good reason why Nobunaga valued Monkey who never got a single samurai head in the battle. This man read Nobunaga's mind. Kicho welcomed the cool breeze, which came into the hall packed with men.

*

In the following June, Yoshi died of illness aged only thirty-three and Yoshi's fourteen year old heir became the Lord of Mino. In February 1562, Yasu[11] from neighboring Mikawa province arrived at Kiyosu to arrange a treaty with Nobunaga. Yasu's retainers were tense. On the eve of the Battle of Okehazama, Yasu invaded Nobunaga's fort at the border and killed the younger Sakuma who was Nobunaga's senior retainer and friend. Nobunaga cheerfully took his long and short swords off his belt and handed them to his page. He then walked straight to Yasu who was surrounded by his fully armed guards.

"Recognize me?"

"Lord Nobunaga, you *are* looking great."

Nobunaga wore a white kimono and black hakama trousers with golden Oda crests. He had an immaculate samurai hairstyle.

"Ha, ha—I don't look like the Fool[12] that you remember?"

---

11 Yasu=Ieyasu Tokugawa

12 The people in Owari used to call him Utsuke, which meant empty head or a fool.

"No, but, I do recognize you, of course."

Yasu smiled in the same way as before—the way of a younger brother admiring the older. Nobunaga entertained Yasu with a tea ceremony. Instead of the traditional private tea room, he took the mob of samurai to a larger tatami room, where Yasu's armed samurai body guards were also invited to attend. When Nobunaga's sister Ichi came in, Yasu's guards gasped unanimously. Her outfit was exquisite. Wearing only light make up, the fifteen year old Ichi had natural porcelain skin and clear almond eyes.

Kicho asked Ichi later on the day, "What did you think of the young samurai from Mikawa?"

"Lord Yasu? He was rude to stare at me!"

"He could not keep his eyes off you, Ichi. Can anyone blame him?"

"Sister Kicho, please stop it. I know what you are going to say—union by marriage, am I right?"

"Yasu has not gone back to his wife since the Battle of Okehazama two years ago. His forging a treaty with us practically cancels his ties with Imagawa and his wife, the niece of late Imagawa Yoshimoto."

"Unless his divorce becomes official, I cannot marry him. Besides, he is shorter than me."

"There aren't many taller than you, my dear . . . You are not in love with another, Ichi, are you?"

Ichi looked away.

This year, Nobunaga's eldest daughter and Yasu's eldest son were engaged. They were both five. Kicho would later learn the real reason why Ichi did not want Yasu.

*

Cherry blossom buds were growing more plump day by day in the castle courtyard. Nobunaga turned to Kicho.

"This will be the last time we see them at Kiyosu Castle."

"We shall see the blossom at Mount Komaki next year?"

"You don't mind moving?"

Kicho chuckled.

"I have given up saying 'no' to you, my lord."

"Remember how much fuss they made when we moved from Nagoya to Kiyosu?"

"Unlike me who comes from Mino, the retainers of the Oda household have a community network, you see. They don't want to leave their relatives and friends."

"I know."

"They have never heard of Mount Komaki. It is a foreign land for them. You might as well say you move to Mount Ninomiya."

"That is a good idea."

Kicho laughed. "I was only joking, my lord. Mount Ninomiya is even further away."

"That is exactly . . ."

Kicho saw Nobunaga's eyes twinkle.

*

On the next day, Nobunaga climbed Mount Ninomiya. He was accompanied by boys from Mino including Kicho's brothers Toshiaki and Shingoro. Everyone thought he was out for an excursion. Because Mount Ninomiya was in the middle of nowhere, no one thought he was serious about moving his headquarters there. The next day, Nobunaga climbed Mount Ninomiya again. This time he had Hayashi, Sakuma, and Shibata as well as five samurai from Mino. Mori, Inaba, Sakai, Makimura and Aoki had become Nobunaga's retainers at the time of Lord Viper's retirement or his death.

"Look at this nice flat piece of land, Hayashi. I give my permission for you to build your residence, here. That area with a big pine tree is suited for you, Sakuma, and that over there will be yours, Shibata." When Nobunaga gave instructions for the residential allotment for senior retainers, they looked at each other. "Do you think he is serious?"

That evening, their wives were upset.

"No way we'll move to Mount Ninomiya."

"It's in the middle of nowhere."

"How can we take our furniture there?"

"There is no road or path."

The next day, when Nobunaga was getting changed to attend the gun squad training, Kicho said,

"I thought Mount Ninomiya was the best location for the new castle, but, everyone complains about it. Would you reconsider Mount Komaki?"

"Mount Komaki?"

"A river goes there from Kiyosu, you see. The transportation is much better."

"Is that so?"

Nobunaga's young pages spread the words quickly. Soon, Hayashi and Sakuma, both looking serious, were on their way to see Nobunaga. They had the difficult task of persuading Nobunaga to change his mind to move to Mount Komaki instead of Mount Ninomiya. When Nobunaga reluctantly agreed, everyone in the Oda household cheered.[13]

*

Nobunaga fought a series of smaller battles with Kicho's nephew, Tatsuoki, during that year. He lost more battles than he won. Strategically moving his headquarters to Mount Komaki, closer to the border, Nobunaga at least showed that he had not forgotten Kicho's father's bequest.

Construction of the castle at Mount Komaki progressed. At the following cherry blossom season, Nobunaga welcomed Kicho to a new palace. It consisted of many tatami rooms partitioned by artistically painted fusuma sliding doors.

"How beautiful."

"I'm going to get the wives and children of our retainers to move here to construct houses and shops at the foot of the mountain."

"I am speechless, my lord. There are so many rooms in my palace quarter, Mother and Ichi can have their own quarters."

"Good. Your nephew Tatsu will think that I've given up on the construction of a fort at Sunomata at Mino's border."

---

13 Shincho koki Nakagawa Taiko p.96.

"Sakuma and Shibata have both failed that task, prevented by Saito's troops, so, you've given up and constructed your headquarters here instead, isn't it right?"

"That's what most people would think . . . ha, ha . . ."

"I stand here and can view Okuchi Castle twenty kilometres away—inside the gate and all."

"Ha, ha. The samurai in Okuchi Castle won't be able to defend themselves any more. They will soon concede and run away to Inuyama Castle without a battle."

"You had a fierce battle at Okuchi Castle, last June . . ."

"I charged in leading the pack of men. Iwamuro Nagato died shielding me. He was speared through his temple." Nobunaga looked up at the cherry blossom. "I don't want any more death, you know."

"On the eve of the Battle of Okehazama, Iwamuro and four other men ran with you before anyone else got up. I haven't seen the gang for some time now."

"I dismissed them."

"Beg your pardon?"

"They complained that I valued Mino samurai and made them my eldest son's retainers while I gave Owari samurai to the second son."

"Dismissed? Your fierce body guards, who were as though your arms and legs?"

"Don't speak so loud." Nobunaga looked around and talked softly into Kicho's earlobes. "Dismissal is on record only."

"Oh?" Kicho enjoyed the sensation in her earlobes. She felt the urge to embrace him, but he did not seem to share the emotion.

Nobunaga said casually, "Obliging Yasu will pick up the unemployed, ha, ha."

"You sent them to Yasu to keep an eye on him?"

Kicho saw Nobunaga's eye reflect the colours of the rainbow. The castle garden was not yet completed, but newly planted young cherry trees were starting to bloom here and there. She stood among the trees wearing a white and green kimono with pink cherry blossoms.

"My lord, this palace has so much space. May I ask for a cottage, for Kitsuno?"

"Kitsuno?"

"She is the birth mother of Toku, the princess to confirm the treaty with Yasu. After giving three children to us, Kitsuno developed puerperal fever, so I gave her leave. She lives back at her home now, but, we should treat her with more respect for the sake of Toku's happiness and a successful treaty with Yasu."

"Kitsuno will be delighted. Let her know straight away."

The next day, Kicho said hesitantly to Nobunaga,

"Kitsuno's brother sent a messenger who says that she may not be well enough to come to the castle. She has been bedridden."

"I had no idea . . ."

Nobunaga jumped on a brown horse. His bodyguards chased after him. At Kitsuno's brother's residence, Nobunaga ignored the gate keeper's earnest greetings and went straight to Kitsuno's room. The house looked just as well maintained as it had been four years ago.

"Lord Nobunaga is here!" Kitsuno heard someone call from a distance. When she heard footsteps, a tall man's shadow appeared behind her shoji sliding doors.

"How are you feeling, Kitsuno?" The shoji was open and Nobunaga sat beside her.

"Lord Nobunaga? Is this a dream?" Kitsuno struggled to get up. "How kind of you to visit me—a sick and useless concubine."

She tried to smile, but tears ran freely.

"I am sorry to neglect you for so long." Nobunaga held her hand.

Kitsuno's brother, who just came in, wiped the corner of his eye.

"I am sorry—to be in futon without any make up."

"Do not worry, Kitsuno. You are the mother of my three children. Come to Mount Komaki Castle. It is not far from here. Kicho sent her koshi carriage for you. We'll find the best doctor in Owari."

"My lady has forgiven me?" As she put her palms together, Kitsuno's tears fell on her hands.

Kitsuno lived within Mount Komaki Castle at her cottage, but, she never recovered. Nobunaga was away at a battle when she died three years later on 13th May, 1566. She was thirty-nine.

*

When the other maids went away on an errand, Kicho said to Kano,

"I regret killing Kitsuno . . ."

"My lady!" Kano looked around and said, "Your voice is too high."

"I was jealous of her giving my lord three children in three years. I knew my lord visited her too soon after the difficult birth of Toku, but said nothing. The health of concubines was my responsibility, yet I purposefully neglected her. I am a murderer."

"Please stop it, my lady. Kitsuno was just unlucky. I ask you never to repeat this to anyone else." Kano wiped her tears.

"I know." Kicho put her kimono cuff to her face. She was thirty-two and had been married to Nobunaga for seventeen years.

"I know the lord loved Kitsuno, yet, he always treated her as a concubine. She must have loved him also and must have had her torment as a woman, yet she never complained. Losing such a kind soul, what can I do now?"

Kicho turned her face to the courtyard and watched the raindrops on the azalea flowers flickering. The month of the rain was just around the corner.

*

Nobunaga had nicknamed his younger sister Ichi, which meant the market, because she loved to go shopping with Kicho as a toddler. Because Nobunaga made sure all the youths were employed, Owari had become a safe place for women and children. It attracted travelling merchants from various parts of Japan bringing wealth to the district and helped Nobunaga to gather military information.

Kicho had a strange feeling that her maids started to speak unkindly of her beautiful sister-in-law, Ichi, recently. Remembering that it had been a while since Ichi stopped her daily visits to Kicho's lounge, Kicho sent an invitation for Ichi to come and select a roll of material for a new season kimono.

"The standard length material is not long enough for you. You are almost as tall as the lord, aren't you?" Kicho held a length of summer silk against Ichi.

"He teases me that I should have been a man, a tall and strong soldier."

Smiling, Kicho thought that Ichi's waist was thicker than she remembered. She then wondered if Ichi's face was puffed up.

"You have not put on weight, have you?"

"Oh, no, Sister Kicho . . . Do you, do you think, so?"

Ichi's anxiety made Kicho suspicious.

"You are not hiding something from me, are you?"

"Sister . . ."

"What? No period for three months? Ichi, wait a moment."

Kicho got all the maids to sit outside to watch for any unexpected guests. She then led Ichi to the middle of the twenty-tatami mat room. Kicho whispered,

"Pregnant? By whom?" Kicho thought of Shibata, who had been sending her love-letters, but quickly dismissed the idea remembering that he got engaged last month to someone else.

Ichi lifted her eyelashes to glance at Kicho and looked down again.

Kicho's voice was husky. "The man is not . . ."

Ichi looked to the side and quivered her handsome lips similar to her brother.

Kicho thought of all the young men at the castle. She could think of only one man that Ichi idolized since she was a little girl.

"Is the man you love . . ." Kicho pulled Ichi's long kimono sleeve to force her to sit down, as she collapsed to the tatami.

"Is the father of the child . . ." Kicho glared at Ichi. ". . . is it my husband, Lord Nobunaga?" Kicho prayed that she would answer negative. Cicadas were noisy outside in the woods.

"Please, Sister Kicho, oh, please don't be angry with him. Brother visited my room alone regarding the failed marriage proposal to Azai Nagamasa, and . . . I got very emotional." Ichi cried.

Kicho felt as if she was hit with a club. She could barely keep straight.

My husband and sister-in-law betrayed me in concert. Moreover, there is an illegitimate child on the way.

She felt her head spin.

"Does he know about the baby?"

"I haven't had the courage to say . . ."

"No . . ."

"What should I do, Sister Kicho?"

". . . I overlooked the matter . . ."

Kicho said so because it was ultimately the first lady's responsibility to maintain the women's welfare at the castle, including their health and chastity. Ichi might have thought it was an expression of forgiveness. Ichi's watery eyes showed a sign of relief. When Kicho saw the slightest smile on Ichi's face, she remembered that she was barren. She was sorry for herself.

"You must give birth to the child. There is no other way. When is it due?"

"I am not certain, Sister."

"It is nine months from the day, Ichi."

"I know that, but, Sister Kicho . . ." Ichi looked at Kicho through her eye lashes, again.

"Ichi!"

Kicho screamed.

It was not a single night's mistake. They are in love!

Kicho tried not to imagine the intimate hours that the lovers shared—their palms together, legs entwining, and more . . . She wanted to scratch Ichi's porcelain face till it bled.

"Listen, Ichi. You are not allowed to love your brother as a man."

Ichi looked down and said nothing.

"How old do you think you are?"

". . . I turned twenty." Her voice was barely audible.

"Do you realize what you've done?"

". . . I know, Sister Kicho, that I am not allowed to stay at this castle for the rest of my life."

Ichi looked aside and her pretty lips trembled. Kicho thought of the irony that the most beautiful young woman in Owari cannot have the man she loves. She then thought of her and Hide in Mino. When Ichi started to cry Kicho was not sympathetic.

"Listen, Ichi. You must make yourself useful for your brother and marry someone else, understand?"

Ichi nodded without looking up. Higurashi cicadas[14] in the woods of Mount Komaki reminded Kicho that it was the end of summer.

*

Aobato, Japanese Green Pigeon

"My lord, I have to talk." Kicho sat behind Nobunaga who seemed deep in thought facing the courtyard.

"Why do you make such a cross face?" Nobunaga turned his neck.

"It is about Ichi." Kicho heard her voice quiver. The cicadas outside were louder.

"What about her?" Nobunaga looked at the pine tree in the courtyard. There were two aobato[15] pigeons on a branch, snuggling up to each other, as they do every day.

I hate those birds. A cat should get them.

"You know what I am talking about, my lord, don't you?"

---

[14] Higurashi: cicadas in Japan active towards the end of summer.

[15] Japanese green pigeon

Nobunaga looked at Kicho puzzled for a moment, then looked back at the birds.

"Did Ichi say something?"

"Everything."

Nobunaga gasped. "Ichi shall go to the Azais." He glared at the tree and swallowed. His profile was filled with sadness and Kicho knew he at least understood that it was an affair not allowed, even for the most powerful man in Owari.

"The baby will arrive in four months."

"Baby?" Nobunaga turned around, his eyes wide open.

"Didn't you know the consequences?"

The consequences never happened to me!

Kicho was angry and sad at the same time. Nobunaga said,

"We shall get her married before the baby arrives."

"I don't know if there is enough time."

"Well, then, after the childbirth."

"My lord, don't you regret what *you* have done?"

"Umm."

"Are you not sorry?"

"Of course, I am, Kicho." Nobunaga slapped his lap. "I am truly sorry. I apologize. Forgive me. I'll send Ichi to the Azais."

Kicho suspected that he apologized only to curb her anger.

I need to sort out this mess we are in, all the same.

"I recall the young samurai's name as Azai Nagamasa."

"He is a reputable young samurai. I gave a part of my name 'naga' to him several years ago."

"Lord Nagamasa's older sister is my brother Yoshi's widow and mother of Tatsu, my nephew, who is the current Lord of Mino. I hear that Lord Nagamasa led an army to a victory against Rokkaku[16] when he was only fifteen."

"A most capable young man. A suitable husband for Ichi, do you agree?" Nobunaga said brightly.

---

16 A family ruled a district closer to Kyoto.

"The Azai is a noble clan. Lord Nagamasa is two years older than Ichi. They will make a nice couple. The only thing that worries me is—wasn't he engaged?"

"The engagement with a daughter of Rokkaku's senior retainer was broken off. Nagamasa's retainers didn't accept him to be a subordinate to the Rokkaku, you see. Nagamasa's retainers forced Nagamasa's father to retire to break off the engagement."

"It is somewhat similar to the forced retirement that Father suffered in Mino."

"Yes. The retainer's collective powers at times have more authority than the head of the clan. I also could have been forced out of succession by my brother Katsu's retainers, if it wasn't for you and your father."

"The Azais have a close tie with the Asakuras, I understand."

"The former Shogun's brother is now taking refuge with the Asakuras."

"After the former shogun was assassinated, his younger brother Yoshiaki escaped the turmoil. Is it your ambition to assist Yoshiaki to re-establish the government?"

"Me? Assist Yoshiaki?"

"You intend to assist the shogun directly rather than through alliance with the Asakuras, don't you?"

"Do you think so? Ha, ha."

Nobunaga laughed cheerfully. Kicho looked confused. She had intended to give Nobunaga a hard time for his sin, but the topic of the conversation shifted from his affair to Ichi's marriage and then to politics and the re-establishment of order in Japan. Was this Nobunaga's tactic to handle his wife? Perhaps, he knew Kicho's passion for the unification of Japan.

Hesitantly, Kicho asked Nobunaga.

"May I have Ichi's baby?"

"Of course, my dear. As soon as it is born, you'll have a parent's ceremony, just as you did with Tada and Toku."

"Well, I mean, can we pretend that I gave birth?" Kicho watched Nobunaga.

"It would be better for you and Ichi's reputations."

"I love your wisdom." Nobunaga laughed again. "Then, *you* are pregnant."

*

Several weeks passed. Kicho whispered to Kano,

"I have not had my period for two months."

"My . . ."

"I can't believe it, either. It has been eighteen years since marriage, but my breasts are tender and nipples are sensitive." Kicho crossed her arms at the chest and inclined her head.

"Tada is ten. He believed I was his real mother until he was seven, when we invited Kitsuno to live at Mount Komaki Castle. I should be happy for my pregnancy, but, if it is a boy, remembering the bloody fight my lord and Katsu endured, I don't know what to think."

"Hope it will be a girl."

"I do not know if I could possibly love another son as much as I love Tada. Just the thought of being pregnant for another, makes me feel as though I am betraying him. I feel guilty."

"Guilty?"

"Say nothing to the lord until I see a doctor."

The wash women, however, leaked the news and rumour eventually reached Nobunaga.

He chuckled, "Kicho really knows the way."

A few days later, Kicho walked in the yard to find a bloody aobato lying on the ground. When Kicho poked it with a twig, green feathers scattered.

A cat has done it.

Kicho saw her own blood that day.

Miscarriage? The aobato's curse?

Kicho felt ominous and saw a doctor immediately. It was a "phantom" pregnancy.

While I was pretending to be pregnant, my body began to react in the way that I really was. It was not the curse of the bird. I was not pregnant in the first place.

Kicho had the maids to bury the bird behind a bush and placed a small stone.

The lord must not see this.

Kicho knew that Nobunaga would be in a bad mood to see Kicho upset.

I feel as though I am burying my fetus.

When she put her palms together in front of the small grave, tears ran.

I am not allowed to share this sorrow with my husband, who never believed my pregnancy. The single aobato came to perch on the tree. He was alone one day after another.

The lonely bird would know how I feel.

A few weeks later, the aobato brought a new mate and as always, the two birds snuggled up together all day. They did not cheer her up.

*

Ichi was tall, and her swelling belly was not obvious inside her robe for a few more months. No one in Owari was brave enough to talk about Ichi and Nobunaga's relationship. It may have been through maids from Mino who had taken leave that the rumour spread. It had been a while since people stopped calling Nobunaga Lord Fool or "Utsuke" in Japanese, but they started to call him Lord "Tawake". Utsuke and Tawake both meant "fool" in Mino and Owari dialect. Utsuke literally meant empty head while Tawake literally meant a person who divided his paddy field equally to his children. It was customary to give it all to the eldest son so that he bears the responsibility to look after the old parents, thus, Tawake was a person who did what he should not do.

*

Kicho had been in Ichi's room for four hours, which seemed an eternity.

"Ha, ha . . ." Ichi started to pant again.

It is a small penalty to pay for the crime of stealing my husband. My consolation is that the baby will be mine.

A small head covered with black hair showed, went back in and showed again. Once the head was out, the whole body was effortlessly pulled out by the midwife. It was a girl.

The red and blotchy creature smeared with blood cried.

Nobunaga came quickly. Kicho sadly understood his affection for Ichi and vowed to keep a close watch on them until her departure.

"Well done, Ichi." Smiling, Nobunaga extended his hands to meet Ichi's unexpected aggression.

"I am keeping my baby."

"The Azai household will not want a baby."

"I shall not go to them, unless they allow me to take her."

"Don't be silly, Ichi."

"It is my only request in my whole life, please, Brother." Ichi's hair, wet with perspiration stuck to her forehead. Kicho said,

"Trust me, dear. I shall take good care of her." Kicho looked forward to the baby's arrival as her own and even suffered a phantom pregnancy. The little girl, now cleansed, slept peacefully. Kicho thought she was the most adorable creature ever.

Ichi looked at Nobunaga. Her eyes quickly welled. Her weary face with uncombed hair looked sensual.

"Umm . . ." Nobunaga groaned. "If it were a boy, I would have had concerns for its life. In case the alliance deteriorated, the Azais would fear my son might rebel against them. They could kill the boy to stop such motion."[17]

". . . no such fear for a girl."

The little girl then started to cry.

Nobunaga flustered. "Don't you cry, my little one. All right, all right. I will ask the Azais."

"Thank you, Brother. Thank you." Ichi handed the baby to Nobunaga. "I promise to be a good wife and ambassador, I promise."

---

[17] The political marriages and surety were arranged so that the parties would try harder to maintain the alliance for the happiness and the life of loved ones.

"You promised *me* . . ." Kicho swallowed the rest of the words. She sensed that there was a new bond between the new parents—the bond which she could never share.

Nobunaga cradled the small creature in both hands. "We shall call her Cha-cha." The baby sucked Nobunaga's little finger and stopped crying. Nobunaga had the gentlest face that Kicho had ever seen.

*

Kicho had to part with another baby this year. In 1567, nine year old Toku was sent to Mikawa to marry Yasu's son. Farmers, peasants, merchants and labourers sat on both sides of the main road to watch the wedding procession. Contrary to Kicho's heartache, Nobunaga's reputation kept improving.

"Have you ever seen such a beautiful koshi?"

". . . and decorated trunks . . . filled with treasures, of course."

"Look at the distinguished uniforms and the orderly way the samurai march."

"Aren't we lucky to be able to come to watch this without worrying about our house being robbed?"

"The lord controls thieves and highway robbers and make unemployed youth construct roads and bridges."

"The lord removed customs to let us travel freely."

"He's established free trade, unification of coins and measurements and a bookkeeping system. It has become a lot easier for us merchants to trade."

"He talks, dances and mingles with us. He knows what we ordinary folks want."

*

Kicho hardly had time to miss Toku after this wedding. There was Ichi's wedding to come. Azai Nagamasa agreed to the wedding, but it worried Kicho that he had not responded to the proposed date.

Gifu Castle

In the meantime, Nobunaga tried to gain Gifu Castle[18] by negotiation rather than bloodshed. Three west Mino samurai, including Inaba who married Kicho's sister, agreed to become Nobunaga's retainers, though their master and Kicho's nephew Tatsuoki did not. Nobunaga led his troop close to the bottom of Mount Kinka and looked up. The castle stood tall at the top. The distance from the bottom of the mountain and the surrounding woods made it almost impossible to attack without suffering many casualties.

When he returned to Mount Komaki Castle that day, Nobunaga said to Kicho, "If we achieved a surprise attack from the other side of the mountain, I bet they'd concede without a fight."

"I've heard of a secret pathway, leading from the Azai territory, that is, my brother's widow's home."

---

[18] It was actually called Inabayama Castle, then, and Nobunaga renamed it to Gifu Castle after taking control of it.

"The boys searched, but, it is too bushy, you know. Is there anyone who might know where the path is?"

"My cousin Hide would. He used to travel to Kyoto and back for Father, many times."

"Can you contact him?"

"I hear that he works for Ashikaga Yoshiaki, the former Shogun's younger brother, but I haven't heard from him for eighteen years."

"I shouldn't send him a messenger. The Asakuras would suspect Hide of a non-existent conspiracy to betray. If you sent a messenger to your cousin, it should be fine."

"I'll send my maid to his mother, Lady Maki."

A few days later, Nobunaga said to Kicho,

"Monkey captured a woman servant fleeing the castle at the other side of the mountain. She had not eaten for days and could hardly walk."

"They must all be starving at the castle. May I see her?"

Kicho gave food and clean clothes to this woman. Kicho asked if she would secretly take some food to Lady Ohmi, Kicho's sister-in-law. After a persuasion, Lady Ohmi's former servant agreed. It was better for Lady Ohmi to concede than to die of starvation.

Monkey, named Hideyoshi as samurai, led a troop. Min-min[19] cicadas were deafening in the forest surrounding the castle. While waiting in the shady bush, a trooper's perspiration ran into his eye. Many servants had fled from starvation and nineteen year old Kicho's nephew, Tatsuoki had taken his heavy armour off to lie down. Sake had long disappeared from the cellar and there was nothing to eat. When Hideyoshi yelled, his armed troop rushed in. Once Tatsuoki was captured, the other samurai at the castle surrendered.

*

Kicho climbed to the top of the castle. Nobunaga renamed it Gifu Castle after an ancient Chinese capital and started renovation and restoration straight away.

---

19 Min-min Cicada: cicadas active at the height of summer in Japan.

The scenery hasn't changed since eighteen years ago. I climbed up here with Mother many times and watched Father and Brother march off with their troops. My relatives who lived here have all passed away, except for . . .

Her thoughts were interrupted by a man's voice talking to Kano downstairs. After a while, Kano's clear voice called.

"Hide is here to see you, I will show him to your lounge."

My cousin, whom I was just thinking of.

Kicho went down and looked in her mirror with subtle bellflower patterns.

I don't look too bad, really.

Kicho went into her refurbished lounge filled with the fresh fragrance of Japanese cypress, which was used for quality dwellings. Hide was sitting in the middle of the room with his head bowed.

Thinner hair?

Kicho sat on her designated cushion at the top end of the room. Hide lifted his head, but was unable to find a suitable word of greeting. Kicho chuckled.

"I was fifteen when I saw you last, but now I am thirty-three."

"I can't believe it. You look just the same."

"You were twenty-one, then, so you must be . . ."

"Thirty-nine." Hide said apologetically. Within minutes, Kicho felt as though she had never been away from him.

Footsteps and voices approached and Kano called,

"My lady, your brothers are here."

"Toshiaki and Shingoro! Did you know who's here?"

Astonished Shingoro cried, "Akechi Hide-sama!"

"Do you recognise me? You were about seven and nine when I left the castle,[20]" Hide smiled.

"You taught us to ride a horse," said Toshiaki.

"I remember the time you tried to teach us how to light a matchlock gun,"

"It was so heavy that I could not hold it steady," Shingoro chuckled.

---

[20] It was called Inabayama Castle and Nobunaga renamed it to Gifu Castle when he moved his headquarters there.

"They used to make a thunderous noise."

"They've improved since. Lord Nobunaga uses the gun squad to scare off and disrupt the enemy," said Toshiaki.

"A gun squad of peasant boys can defeat an army of brave horsemen."

"He's changing the way to fight a war. He uses intelligence, spies, negotiations by diplomats."

"Enough about . . ." Kicho was going to remind her younger brothers that Hide no longer belonged to the same household, when Kano announced,

"The Young Lord Strange is here."

Kicho's face lit up. Eleven-year-old Nobunaga's heir arrived with one bony shoulder bare, but he tucked it back into his kimono as he entered Kicho's room.

"Did I interrupt your archery lesson with your father?" Kicho apologized.

"No problem, Mother. Father said I should meet your cousin." Lord Strange nodded. Hide, Toshiaki and Shingoro spontaneously moved down to make a room for the boy at the top end of the room next to Kicho and bowed. Lord Strange returned a bow and sat.

Hide smiled at Kicho, "I was so wrong to fear that you might be lonely. How wonderful to see you surrounded by nice men."

"They are my children, really . . . you have your own family, Hide?"

"I married Tsumaki Hiroko and we have two daughters." Hide did not mention that Hiroko was heavily pregnant with their third.

"How nice." Kicho forced a smile. After a pause, she said,

"Do you mind me asking why you were not at Father's side when he died?"

"Lord Viper sent a messenger to tell me not to get involved in a family conflict. I was sorry for not being able to assist."

"I perfectly understand."

"Lord Nobunaga led his army into Mino, at that time . . ."

"He had a reason."

"Lord Viper's bequest to him, right?" Hide looked away, and bit his lip.

Kicho changed the subject. "Are you here to represent the Asakuras?"

"I am employed by the Asakuras, but . . ." He hesitated.

Kicho looked at the younger men. "Lord Strange, Toshiaki and Shingoro, thank you all for interrupting your schedules to come to see Hide. You may get back to your work now." Kicho gave a special smile to Lord Strange as he left.

He has grown.

Hide straightened himself.

"Can you please introduce me to Lord Nobunaga?"

"Since the coup, which killed the already powerless shogun in Kyoto three years ago, the younger brother of the deceased shogun has been protected by the Asakura clan for three years, I hear. It is easy for me to introduce you to my husband, of course, but may I ask you why?"

"Please, Kicho. The Asakuras need Lord Nobunaga's cooperation to bring order back to Japan."

"My husband also wishes for the restoration of order and the unification of Japan."

"So, he will have an alliance with the Asakuras?"

"I feel that the 'order' he has in his mind is somewhat different from the restoration of the old that you are thinking of."

"In what way?"

"That, you will need to ask my husband yourself . . ."

". . . Do you know why I haven't come to you earlier?"

". . . Were you hesitant, Hide, because of our previous courtship?"

"That as well, but moreover . . . You see, though I receive my income from the Asakuras, I am a direct retainer of Lord Yoshiaki." Hide stuck out his chest. "I have my ambition to control the new shogunate for him."

Kicho gasped. "Ambition to control the . . . of course you do! After all, you were Father's favourite samurai."

I did not want to hear this, thought Kicho.

"I am an honourable retainer of the new shogun to be."

"Please understand, Hide. My husband has been the lord of the castle since the age of two. He has never worked for someone else and does not know how to. I am happy to introduce you to my husband, if you understand this. Besides," Kicho breathed in. "You did not marry me when you should have."

"Please don't . . . ," Hide flustered.

"Father would have made me your bride if you wished. He just did not want to use me to tie you down."

*

Hide returned to Mino in 1568 on a secret mission of the would-be shogun. He had a document which stated that Ashikaga Yoshiaki entrusted Nobunaga to re-establish the shogunate.

Gifu Castle's restoration progressed and the first floor consisted of twenty rooms divided by polished corridors and fusuma sliding doors, artistically painted by Kano Eitoku. Hide was in the formal lounge adorned with an engraved porch and gold edged fusuma. He sat at the top end of the room as the shogun's representative, expecting Nobunaga to kowtow flat on tatami to receive the document. Nobunaga had not arrived.

There was a bustle of hammers and planes mingling with the cries of Higurashi cicadas outside. Labourers carrying timber yelled to time and encourage the activities. There was a fresh fragrance of conifer timber in the air.

Mori Yoshinari[21] finally appeared. He was polite towards Hide who was dressed in *hitatare*[22] as the shogun's representative.

"I seek your forgiveness for making a shogun's official wait. Lord Nobunaga, however, is at his lady's lounge. He says that he wishes to meet the lady's cousin before he has the pleasure of meeting the shogun's messenger."

"I don't understand." Hide tilted his neck. "I *am* the shogun's representative and the lady's cousin. You know that, Mori-san." Mori and Akechi Hide were colleagues in Lord Viper's days.

---

21 http://ja.wikipedia.org/wiki/%E6%A3%AE%E5%8F%AF%E6%88%90 accessed 1/8/11

22 Formal court robe of samurai. Two pieces.

"Please accept my sincere apology for your inconvenience. Lord Nobunaga, however, is in his lady's lounge. He asks the shogun's representative to wait a little longer."

"I concede."

"This way, please, sir."

When they were out in the gallery, Mori was full of chummy smiles. "How're you? Long time no see!" In Lord Viper's days, Mori and Hide were both Kicho's admirers along with many other samurai in Mino. Mori first went to Owari as Lord Viper's secondment, but, after Lord Viper's death, he chose to stay with Nobunaga. It had been thirteen years since he became one of Nobunaga's most trusted retainers.

Guiding along the long gallery which surrounded the first floor of the Castle, Mori explained proudly.

"Lord Nobunaga is constructing the second floor as the lady's residence and the third floor for the tea ceremony rooms. Where I am taking you is just a temporary lounge."

From the gallery, Hide looked down to see the carpenters move busily on the ground. Far away at the bottom of the mountain, there also seemed to be a major housing estate on the way. Mori kneeled in front of Kicho's room.

"My lady, I have brought Akechi Hide-san."

Kicho was sitting at the top of the lounge wearing a brilliant kimono gown. The seat next to her was vacant. Hide sat on the lower ranking side of the room facing her. It is a habit as it was in Lord Viper's days.

"My husband was looking forward to seeing you," Kicho bowed graciously.

The sound of footsteps approached from the porch and a man wearing a casual cotton kimono stood. He threw his long legs out and sat cross legged next to Kicho. He loosened his kimono collar and fanned himself to cool down. Before Hide had a chance to compose himself,

"I am Nobunaga. Good to meet you."

"How do you do, sir?"

"Are you the Asakura's retainer or the shogun's?"

"I am a direct retainer of shogun, however, I receive income from the Asakuras, sir."

"The shogun has no resource to pay you."

"That is correct, sir."

"How much do you get from the Asakuras?"

"Well . . ." Hide was bewildered. Not a minute had passed since he met this man.

"You don't want to say?"

Hide searched for an appropriate word.

"Then, I'll ask," Nobunaga said, "Can you be my retainer for ten thousand bushels?"

"Sir," spontaneously, Hide bent forward to kowtow. He was astounded. His income from the Asakuras was not even half of this. Nobunaga had a spy to investigate.

"Good. Your first job is to bring Lord Ashikaga Yoshiaki secretly to Mino. Can you do it?"

"Yes, sir," bowing low, Hide concealed his face bursting with laughter. It was too easy. Yoshiaki's letter proposed Nobunaga exactly that—*discreetly*, that is, without waiting for an agreement with the Asakuras, who he stayed and negotiated with for three long years with no progress towards unification of war-torn Japan.

Nobunaga promised, "My sister Ichi shall marry Azai Nagamasa to confirm our alliance with the Azais, who have a traditional connection with the Asakuras, in order to curb the Asakura's objection."

"Sir."

"By the way, I must meet the shogun's representative, now. I thought it was more important to meet you, the cousin of my wife, first, Hide-san."

"Yes, sir."

Hide did not quite comprehend what Nobunaga meant, but as he made a bow he realized that he had become Nobunaga's retainer, within a few minutes of meeting him. He did not regret it, however. Ten thousand bushels—Hide imagined Hiroko's delighted face. She had given birth to their third daughter last month and it would be nice to afford a babysitter. Devoted Hiroko had endured a lonely life in Mino for ten years while he served the shogun in Kyoto. Hide just needed polite excuses for the Asakuras.

"If you excuse me," Nobunaga stood. "I must go." He walked away in long strides.

Hide watched Nobunaga's back forgetting to kowtow.

Kicho bowed gracefully. "I introduced my husband to you as I promised. He is a busy person, but please feel free to come and see me at any time. I know you wish to re-establish the Akechi clan and its Lordship. It is my wish also."

When Hide went outside, Mori was waiting. Mori showed him to the great hall and announced,

"The representative of the shogun!"

The hall was packed with formally dressed Oda household samurai kowtowing flat on tatami. Mori showed Hide to the head seat facing them. Hide took time to sit down and composed himself.

"You may raise your faces."

A man immaculately dressed in hitatare at the top of all retainers slowly lifted his face.

"When did he get changed?" astounded Hide. It was Nobunaga.

**

The Asakuras were not happy but could not reasonably declare a war against the shogun who had lived with them for three years. On September 7th, 1568, Nobunaga farewelled the shogun in Mino and immediately started negotiations with warlords in the vicinity. Within a week, Nobunaga conquered all the resisting forces in Ohmi. He sent a messenger to the shogun requesting him to join the battle to push ahead to claim Kyoto. The shogun was hesitant, afraid of the danger. Everything happened too fast for him.

Kicho went to the Rissho temple to persuade the shogun.

"Please speak to the shogun for me." Without a title she was not allowed to speak to him directly. "My husband has conquered Ohmi and it is quite safe to travel even for a woman like me. I will help you prepare for your trip and accompany you," she had an official to relay what she said.

Reluctantly, the shogun agreed to depart Mino. Nobunaga crossed Lake Biwa on September 26 and the shogun followed him the next day.

Everyone who joined the force with Nobunaga thought it was an honour that they would proudly tell generations of descendants. According to Shincho Koki, their spirit was renewed daily, the force had an energy equal to a great river flood. In southern Ohmi, Nobunaga conquered the Rokkaku clan, and demanded Matsunaga and Imai each surrender their treasured tea containers to show their obedience.[23]

On October 14, Nobunaga welcomed the Shogun Yoshiaki to Kyoto. On October 22, the emperor pronounced Yoshiaki as the fifteenth Shogun of the Ashikaga Shogunate. Yoshiaki asked Nobunaga to be the vice-shogun, but he declined.[24]

"Don't you think you upset Lord Yoshiaki by declining the offer?"

Kicho asked Nobunaga.

"The Takedas, the Uesugis, the Asakuras and the Mohris—all the major warlords will be jealous of me, don't you think? I am scared of them more than Yoshiaki."

"True. They all have Genji bloodline or the shogunate's heritage, as well. My lord, everything went too well, too fast. I feel as though I am dreaming, still."

"The shogun wanted me to give me a property in Osaka[25], but . . ."

"Please don't decline the offer, my lord. It is a token reward. It is rude to decline."

"I don't want anything from him. I'm not his retainer."

"Then, please accept it in my name"

"Sure. You can have it."

"I am honoured. In case you abandon me, it will come in handy."

"I will never abandon you, silly . . . but I may die in a battle at any . . ."

Kicho sealed Nobunaga's lips with hers. She did not want to be reminded.

---

23 Shincho Koki

24 Shincho Koki

25 It was called Sakai at the time. See Shincho Koki re lady Nobunaga's property managed by Matsui Yukan.

Only six days after the re-establishment of the Ashikaga Shogunate, Kicho and Nobunaga left Kyoto to return to Gifu. On October 27th, they lodged at Joubodaiin Temple together.[26]

They were served vegetarian meals at the Buddhist temple. They had ripened persimmons for supper. It was Kicho's favourite.

"You need two hands," holding the slippery fruit, Kicho giggled. Sharing sweets with her cheerful husband all to herself was as exciting as the re-establishment of the shogunate for her.

"You cannot eat this in front of the shogun," Kicho kissed him and Nobunaga chuckled. Crickets sounded far away from the mosquito net covering their futon.

"Joubodaiin is not in the middle of the high mountain, but just having Mount Ibuki behind, it has the same serene atmosphere."

"I was entertained by the Azais here, on the way to Kyoto."

". . . The Azai's senior retainer, Endo tried to assassinate you then, right?"

"I was cautious, so Endo had no chance. Azai Nagamasa had no idea about Endo's plan."

"I have some doubts, my lord."

"I trust Azai Nagamasa. He and Ichi love each other, you see."

". . . Is it true that you and Ichi 'talked' all night by yourselves here that night?"[27]

"Who told you that?" Nobunaga turned with eyes wide open.

"So, my ninja was right!" Kicho pinched him.

"Stop it. It hurts. I never did what you are thinking of. We had so much to talk about, you see. Believe me."

"Even if I believed you, consider what they thought at the Azai household. If I heard the rumour, Lord Nagamasa must have heard it too. Consider how he felt."

"I am sorry, I apologise," said Nobunaga, bashing his lap and bowing at the same time.

How many times do I accept his 'apology'?

---

26 Akechi Chronicle. Shincho Koki only mentions Nobunaga's stay and omitted to mention that Kicho was with him.

27 Azai Chronicle

"I am not talking about *my* forgiveness. I am talking about *Lord Nagamasa*'s feelings. It was not permissible behaviour, was it?"

"It is why you are here with me tonight to make sure I behave this time and save my reputation, my dear lady?"

"Do you trust Lord Nagamasa?"

"Yes. He loves Ichi."

"Well . . ."

"Your father Lord Viper trusted me knowing we loved each other. Isn't that right?"

"I hope you are right, my lord."

Love for Ichi cannot guarantee Nagamasa's faithfulness for the Oda clan. While Ichi was engaged to Nagamasa, my husband seduced her. Even if Nagamasa tried to forget, every time he looks at Baby Cha-cha, he will be reminded. I should have insisted on keeping Cha-cha with me. Nobunaga thinks he showed his trust by giving Nagamasa his beloved sister and his baby as well, but I don't know if Nagamasa shares the same sentiment. He would have complex feelings about this.

Kicho and Nobunaga left Joubodaiin Temple the next day, October 28 1568. Under the typical blue sky of autumn, excited residents lined up on either side of the highway to welcome the heroes. Thirty-five year old Nobunaga looked handsome wearing a white war-jacket with the golden Oda crest. He trotted a decorated horse in the front of Kicho's lacquered koshi. The farmers and peasants cheered. The first step to mark the end the civil war in Japan was achieved by the samurai and foot soldiers of Gifu and Owari, led by the husband of the Mino Princess. It was an honour belonging to all who lived in the Nobi (Mino-Owari) plain.

*

In the new year of 1569, on January 6, the roof of Gifu Castle was white with snow which had been falling since the night before. Lord Nobunaga was relaxing in Kicho's private lounge playing go[28] with the

[28] Japanese chess like game, played with black and white tablets.

twelve year old Lord Strange and eleven year old Lord Tea-whisk.[29] His third son Lord Three-seven was not there because when Nobunaga conquered Ise in the previous year, he was sent there with an agreement to marry the daughter of the head samurai and become the heir of the clan.

With her hands over a hibachi[30] Kicho was looking at the unusually heavy snow fall. She turned to Nobunaga.

"You had your initiation at thirteen and battle induction at fourteen, right?"

"Umm." Nobunaga said lifting a black go piece.

"Lord Strange will be thirteen next year, you know."

At that moment, a page ran in and said,

"Akechi Hide has sent an urgent messenger from Kyoto."

"Show him," Nobunaga said, and a messenger ran into the courtyard. He tried to kneel down, but slipped forward on snow. Before he had time to apologise and re-compose, Nobunaga urged,

"What happened?"

The messenger's face was soiled and white snow covered his shoulders.

"Tatsu,[31] Nagai, [32] and Miyoshi's coalition have invaded Lord Ashikaga Yoshiaki's residence."

"What?"

"My nephew and Nagai . . . whose lives I begged you to spare . . . I am so sorry, I had no idea." Kicho had not communicated with them since the time they fled Gifu two years ago.

"Be quiet." Nobunaga stood waving his hands to Kicho and rushed to the veranda. The messenger's breathing barely settled but he explained as he gasped for more air.

"They, have, almost reached the shogun's palace."

---

29 Nobunaga nick named him this because his second son had a lot of hair as a baby.

30 a large container used for heating and boiling water.

31 Saito Tatsuoki: Kicho's nephew. Kicho's half-brother Yoshi(tatsu)'s heir.

32 Nagai Michitoshi: Some sources say he was Kicho's uncle, others say Kicho's half-brother born before Lord Viper married Kicho's mother.

"I'm going," said Nobunaga to Kicho, who had already packed his clothes. Nobunaga looked as though he was determined to set off even if it was by himself and he jumped on the horse. The men in charge for horses carrying goods and arms started to quarrel. Nobunaga jumped off his horse and checked each one of the loads.

"I can't tolerate unequal treatment by the person in charge." Large flakes of snow fell and stayed on his eyelashes and eyebrows.

"The loads are all the same, hurry," he declared and off he went.[33] His young pages chased after him. Many horses hesitated to gallop on the snowy surface. Some slipped and even broke legs. From Gifu to Kyoto, in good weather, it usually took at least three days. Nobunaga ran through in two days in heavy snow. When he left there were two hundred horsemen chasing him, but, there were only ten who ran into Kyoto with him.[34] Ten horsemen poured into the palace in one bundle. The teenage pages who managed to keep up with Nobunaga were all red faced and breathless. Nobunaga alone was cool and collected, with piercing eyes.

*

Just before Nobunaga's arrival, Hide and Nagamasa's coalition managed to chase the enemy away. The rumour that Nobunaga had left Gifu and was fast approaching was enough to scare the enemy's mercenaries.

Nobunaga decided, "The shogun needs a secure palace." He urged all the allies and conquered lords to send labourers and goods to contribute for the construction of the new palace for the shogun. Nobunaga chose an old residential[35] site at Nijo in Kyoto and immediately had the labourers start digging deep moats. After consulting Hide and the Imperial Court, Nobunaga selected an auspicious day to mark the ground breaking ceremony for the palace. He visited the site daily himself to direct the team of builders and urged them to hurry.

---

33 Shincho Koki

34 Shincho Koki

35 The old residence belonged to the Shiba clan was in Nijo area in Kyoto. See Shincho Koki.

Kicho arrived at Kyoto after the snow season. Nobunaga asked, "You have never seen a *red-hair*,[36] have you?"

"Is it true that they have red skin, long noses and look as terrible as a *tengu*?[37]"

"I saw one hiding behind the hall full of retainers. He was just a human, actually. He spoke our language."

"Really?"

"He comes by sea from a land further away than China. His courage to risk his life for his beliefs deserves my respect. He says the earth is a globe, which makes sense to me. I'm going to meet with a *red-hair* called Frois[38] to show him the construction site. Come at the hour of the horse,[39] dressed as a tourist."

Kicho shared an unremarkable hired koshi with Kano. She had a long veil draped over her hat and face, following the custom among decent women in Kyoto in those days. Nobunaga was there already, walking with a Portuguese missionary, Luis Frois, who was as tall as Nobunaga, well-built, and wore a long black robe.

His robe has no front layers. He is wearing a long necklace with a cross. He has red-brown hair, red skin and a long nose, like a tengu . . .

Kicho started to stroll. Labourers kept working hard under Nobunaga's watch, taking no notice of Kicho or the *red-hair.* A young labourer stood suddenly, walked towards Kicho and gave her an indecent grin. Before she had time to do anything, he ripped her veil off to look at her face.

Nobunaga saw this misbehaviour some fifteen metres away and walked towards the man in long strides. The man saw Nobunaga coming and started to run in the opposite direction, but, Nobunaga was faster.

Nobunaga swayed his long sword behind the offender. "Die." With a little spray of blood, the head of the man flew away from his body and rolled onto the site. The head had eyes wide open in disbelief. They begged Kicho to agree it was not real. She looked away. Kano picked up Kicho's blood-spattered veil and helped her to replace it on her hat.

---

[36] Red-hair people = term used to refer to Europeans in 16c Japan.

[37] A fictional character with super natural powers, in Japanese fairy tales.

[38] A Portuguese missionary Luis Frois. Author of the History of Japan.

[39] Between 11am and 1pm.

Nobunaga's page did not waste time in ordering some of the men to take away the body parts, which had started to ooze fresh blood from the neck. Another page wiped Nobunaga's sword with *Kaishi*[40] paper and Nobunaga inserted it back into its case on his waist band. Without a glance at Kicho or the body, Nobunaga returned to Frois, who later documented the incident.

If Frois thought Nobunaga was a merciless tyrant, Kicho thought otherwise.

A woman wearing a veil was obviously a person with a status if not Nobunaga's wife. The man must have had motives other than to tease a woman. If my husband did not do what he had done, I may have had to kill him in self-defence. If my face became known to many in the process, I would no longer be able to walk in the city of Kyoto among the citizenry.

The leafless plum trees, which Nobunaga planted on the site, had deep pink blossoms; spring was near.

*

While he oversaw the construction work, Nobunaga had Kicho purchase valuable tea ceremony utensils and artworks from the wealthiest merchants of Sakai, now Osaka.[41] As he used rice, gold and silver as currency and in turn imposed taxes on the merchants, it helped to spread the wealth to the ordinary citizens. After three months, the palace was furnished and Kicho and Nobunaga returned to Gifu.[42] Because Nobunaga did not tolerate stealing, rape or any other misbehaviour, Kyoto became a safe place for women and children. Shops, temples and shrines in Kyoto prospered with many tourists.

Gifu Castle's refurbishment progressed and Nobunaga was ready to construct the palace quarters for Kicho. Kicho's sister-in-law Lady Ohmi still stayed with her, but after Kicho's nephew Tatsuoki rebelled against the new shogunate, Nobunaga became unhappy with Lady

---

[40] Traditional pocket tissues.
[41] Shincho Koki
[42] Shincho Koki

Ohmi. He then remembered about a tea container that Lord Viper bequest him.

"It is a tea container with an engraved writing of *tenkabufu,* meaning samurai's rule. Lord Viper entertained me with it just before the Battle at Muraki Castle in 1554. I liked it and Lord Viper offered it to me, but I said, 'It is too much a burden for me at present', Lord Viper then said, 'I will mind it until the day you unify Japan.'"

"I remember, but, Lady Ohmi says it was lost in the battle."

"It can't be. The Oda soldiers never steal."

"I know, but, we have searched everywhere."

"She is hiding it. She doesn't want to give it to me."

"Lady Ohmi is not only Tatsuoki's mother, but also my sister-in-law and the older sister of Azai Nagamasa, Ichi's husband. She would never hide such a thing. She says if you won't forgive her, she will commit suicide to bear the blame."

"Good," said Nobunaga. "I grant my permission. She's just saying that so I'll give up pursuing it."

"She feels you are blaming her for her son's coup. All her relatives, as many as sixteen women including my nieces and grandnieces say they will follow her if she dies. Think about it, my lord. It would upset Azai Nagamasa and Ichi's relationship."

He has got abundant treasures of the tea ceremony utensils from Kyoto. Why is he so obsessed about a humble tea cup of Father's?

Kicho became desperate.

"Very well, my lord. I am also her relative. I am going to commit suicide with her to share the blame."

"What?"

"You don't need me. Mrs Saucepan will look after you." Kicho forgot she vowed never to complain about his concubines.

"All right, Kicho. I will forgive your sister-in-law, so, don't ever talk about suicide."

Kicho sighed in relief, but Nobunaga said,

"Only one thing, though. Are they your true relatives? Was Yoshi your real brother and your father's son? Is Tatsu, whose life I had spared, your real nephew?"

"I believe so."

"Can you prove it?"

"No one can prove it, now."

"There is a way."

"Is there?"

"The person who gave birth to Yoshi would know."

"You mean Father's former concubine?"

"That's right. We will ask Miyoshino."

"Are you going to get her to come to you?"

"It is probably better if I went to see her. If I treated her with respect, I think she would tell me the truth. After all, I'm asking her past affairs."

"Let me ask her, my lord. She would be more comfortable with a woman."

"I want to hear it directly from her."

Kicho whispered something and Nobunaga grinned.

Kicho got into her koshi which climbed down the long decending path of Mount Kinka. A samurai servant in unremarkable attire followed her koshi. Min-min cicadas were noisy in the forest and reminded Kicho of the hot day Tatsu [43] left Gifu Castle two years ago. Miyoshino lived at the foot of the mountain. There was a large bush of hydrangea with purple flowers at the entrance of the humble house.

"Princes Kicho, beg your pardon, Lady Kicho. What a nice surprise." Miyoshino bowed and invited in Kicho and her samurai servant carrying a large parcel inside.

"How are you Mother?"

"How kind of you to call me Mother. I feel honoured."

"You are Brother Yoshi's mother, so you *are* my mother. Mother, I never forget the heartache you must have endured since I left Mino. Please let me know if I can make your life any easier. I brought kimono materials for you, today."

The samurai servant bowed courteously and placed rolls of kimono materials in front of Miyoshino.

"Wait in the next room," Kicho ordered the samurai servant.

---

43 Her nephew, Lady Ohmi's son, who rebelled against the new shogun since he left Gifu.

". . . my lady." He bowed low and Kicho grinned. He was Nobunaga dressed as her servant.

"I am always grateful for your kindness. These are too good for me, really."

"When I saw them in a little shop in Kyoto, I thought they would look nice on you, Mother . . . I came here today to ask you something that I have wanted to know for a long time. It is regarding Brother Yoshi's birth."

Miyoshino was silent.

"You may wonder why I ask, after all these years, but I need to know if he was Father's real son."

"I am sorry, but, I am unable to answer . . ."

"Forgive me to be rude and ask about the relationship between you and Father, but it is very important for me to know whether Brother Yoshi was my blood brother."

Miyoshino said nothing.

"Brother Yoshi and I grew up in the same castle. He was kind to me. Then, I went to Owari to marry Lord Fool . . ."

Nobunaga cleared his throat in the adjoining room. Kicho paused for a moment but continued,

"I regret that Brother Yoshi and I became enemies since, but I had no option but to follow my husband's path."

"I know exactly how you must have felt. I endured the same heartache when Lord Viper and my son became enemies."

"My husband kindly spared the life of Tatsuoki, your grandson and my nephew. Most Mino samurai have now become my husband's retainers. My husband has moved his headquarters to Gifu, wishing to live with my relatives amicably . . . Brother Yoshi was born eight months after you became Father's, is that right?"

Miyoshino looked away.

"Was Brother Yoshi Father's son or was he the former lord's son?"

Miyoshino bit her lips.

"Please, Mother, I need to know." Kicho bowed slowly and kept her head low. The Min-min cicadas cried outside, but not a sound came from the adjoining room where Nobunaga waited. When Kicho finally raised her face with a sound of silk kimono sleeves rustling, her eyes met the moist eyes of Mother.

"When I became Lord Viper's concubine, I had no relationship with the previous lord for more than a year."

"Brother Yoshi, then, is Father's . . ."

"There is no doubt at all."

Kicho breathed out in relief.

Miyoshino said, "Yoshi's coup, a son against his father, should never have happened. Yoshi decided to believe that Lord Viper was not his father for political reasons. It was heart wrenching for me. Lord Viper never denied, hoping his son better support from Mino samurai, if they believed he was the rightful lord. Lord Viper died with the secret to protect his son." Miyoshino sobbed.

"Father loved him, I know. We were once a happy family. I remember the time he took me horse riding and fishing . . . and shopping at the market . . . those memories seem to be a dream now."

"One day, we might have a peaceful nation where no one needs to kill for survival." Miyoshino looked afar and unwittingly glared at the space where Nobunaga waited. Cicadas were suddenly louder and Kicho felt oily perspiration in her arm pits.

Miyoshino, who never met Nobunaga, had no idea who he was. Kicho composed herself.

"I never wanted to be Brother's enemy. Please understand that I just could not let anyone murder my husband."

"I know, dear Kicho." Miyoshino nodded putting her kimono sleeve to her eye.

Kicho heard Nobunaga move in the adjoining room, but she did not care. She thought it was a chance to make him listen. "I brought up my little sisters and arranged their marriages to Mino samurai to gain their cooperation and obedience. It was necessary to stop them trying to murder my husband."

"I understand."

"Father's words of prediction that my brothers will one day be Nobunaga's retainers became reality by Shingoro and Toshiaki, but Brother Yoshi was different . . ."

"Yoshi grew up as Lord Viper's successor, you know. He was upset by Lord Viper's words."

"I understand. He also had the support of many Mino samurai who believed he was the son of the former lord whom Father displaced."

". . . I nearly forgot, dear Lady Kicho. I have something that Lord Viper asked me to keep for your husband."

"He did?"

"It is a tea container. I will go and fetch it."

Miyoshino stood and then was gone. Nobunaga danced into the room. "Well done, Kicho!"

"No, go back, please."

"It doesn't matter now, Kicho. You've done everything perfectly."

"Please wait. I cannot embarrass Miyoshino.

"But, Kicho . . ."

"Go back, servant." Kicho scolded him.

Reluctantly, Nobunaga went and Miyoshino returned with a box wrapped in a dusty cloth.

"Oh," Kicho recognised the tea container. "Thank you Mother, thank you." Unwittingly raising her voice, Kicho heard Nobunaga rustling in the adjoining room. He could never sit still for long. Kicho was tearful at the thought of the tea cup saving many lives.

Miyoshino said, "Lord Viper asked me to keep it until Lord Nobunaga unified Japan. I think Lord Nobunaga deserves it now as he has achieved the re-establishment of the Ashikaga Shogunate. Lord Viper's prediction sounded absurd at the time and he secretly entrusted the container to me. By doing so, he must have hoped that I would encourage Yoshi to concede to Lord Nobunaga, but, you know, my son never listened to me . . ."

Miyoshino seemed to want to talk forever, but Kicho was worried about Nobunaga getting restless. Kicho said a few more kind words to her and stood.

Nobunaga could not wait until they returned to Gifu Castle. He stopped Kicho's koshi in a shade and opened the box. His eyes beamed.

A few days later, Kicho made Nobunaga revisited Miyoshino with gold, silver and rice to thank her for the tea container.[44] Kicho could not tell if Miyoshino recognised him from the other day. The news of Nobunaga paying respect to his mother-in-law, in any case, spread to enhance his popularity.

**

In the following spring of 1570, Kicho made purchases in Sakai and Kyoto for treasures for the tea ceremony. Nobunaga urged the shogun to send requests to the Asakuras to contribute towards the cost of the shogun's palace construction. The Asakuras, with whom the shogun had lodged for three years before meeting Nobunaga, had refused to send labourers for the palace construction. When the Asakuras ignored repeated requests, Nobunaga decided to seek their obedience by force.

Assisted by Yasu's force, Nobunaga chased the Asakuras, winning one battle after another, when suddenly the Azais broke the treaty and attacked the Odas from behind. Nobunaga refused to fight with Ichi's husband and ran away to Kyoto deserting his entire army.

Kicho went back to Gifu and waited nervously for Nobunaga. As the news of his defeat spread, Kyoto and surrounding districts became unstable again. On May 21, 1970, Kano said to Kicho hesitantly,

"The lord was shot . . ."

"What?"

"I do not know the details, but . . ."

"Is he alive!"

"Yes, he has just returned."

"Why didn't you say so, first, you scared me . . ."

"I am sorry, my lady. All I heard was that the lord had avoided the main highway through the Azai territory and was coming home through the mountains and . . ."

---

[44] The Diary of Kototsugu mentions Nobunaga's visit to his mother-in-law, four days after the incident with the tea container. Kicho's mother had passed away by this time, the author presumed her to be Miyoshino.

Kicho ran towards the front of the castle. He got shot, but, he's alive. How bad is the injury? Is his life in danger? Did I get punished for thinking unkindly about him lately?

*

"What's up? You look pale, Kicho."

Nobunaga was in his change room. His face looked a little tanned, but unhurt.

"You're all right, my lord? Where is the wound?"

"My favourite riding jacket got two big holes, see?"

"Oh, no . . ." Kicho put her hand to her mouth. The jacket with burnt holes smelled of gun powder. Nobunaga looked at her amused. She took out some ointment in a clam shell container from the medicine box.

"Please don't move while I do this. You are bleeding on your forearm. You are lucky to be alive! I hear the villain Zenjubo has never missed a target within the distance of twenty metres."

"I am immortal."

"No one is . . ." Kicho swallowed the word.

*

The new shogun was not happy that Nobunaga had actual powers, not he. Encouraged by the win of the Azai and Asakura coalition against Nobunaga, the shogun started to invite other warlords with Genji bloodlines, with connection to the shogun's family, to form an alliance against Nobunaga. Nobunaga needed to do something quickly knowing that his only faithful allies were Yasu and Mituhide.

Chased by Nobunaga, the Azais and the Asakuras retreated into Mount Hiei. Nobunaga reasoned with the priests who provided refuge for them.

"If you are religious, do not take sides in political issues."

The priests of Mount Hiei did not cooperate with Nobunaga, so he ordered Hide to burn the temple.

"There are women and children as well as priceless treasures at the holy temple at Mount Hiei," said Kicho. Upon consulting Kicho's brothers and other academics in Kyoto, Nobunaga said, "I concede."

Nobunaga regretted this decision. Later this year, farmers lead by a religious sect attacked and killed one of Nobunaga's faithful brothers [45] and brother-in-law in Nagashima. Nobunaga did not consult anyone again. He ordered Hide and Monkey to burn the holy temple at Mount Hiei in September, 1972. According to Frois, 1,500 people died.

Kicho would say, "Please think of your reputation in Kyoto." Nobunaga carried out policies to improve the life of the imperial household in Kyoto in an effort to restore his reputation.

For the next eleven years, Nobunaga was forced to fight rebels led by priests and religious leaders in various parts of Japan. Nobunaga permitted Hide to construct a castle at Sakamoto to watch Mount Hiei where the temple used to be.

Kicho congratulated Hide.

"Only four years since you met my husband and you are the first lord of the castle among all retainers."

"Lord Nobunaga treats me as his brother-in-law, thanks to you."

Sakamoto Castle stood by Lake Biwa. Kicho and Nobunaga met Hiroko and Hide's hearty welcome. They walked across the bridge with crimson railings looking down at the colourful fish. Hide took Nobunaga for a tour of other parts of the castle while Hiroko and Kicho sat down.

"The water is like a mirror reflecting the white donjon.[46] I can watch this all day."

"Hide and I are so grateful that Lord Nobunaga treats us as his relatives." Hiroko said holding a tea cup with her delicate fingers.

"My husband regretted not being able to save Akechi Castle, my mother's home. There is also another reason." Kicho looked aside. "During the year that he burned Mount Hiei, one of my maids, Mrs Saucepan got pregnant by him. He built a house at the foot of Mount

[45] Oda Nobuoki

[46] Castle tower

Kinka for her.[47] He must have felt the need to show that he is not neglecting me and my relatives to maintain the cooperation of Mino's samurai. Is it true, Hiroko, that Hide never had a concubine?"

"I had three girls before I gave him an heir, but he never had a concubine," said Hiroko apologetically.

"I made Lord Strange's nurse at Gifu visit my husband's bed."

"You didn't?"

"I thought he liked her and I was right. It was good for Lord Strange who needed to grow up. She had a girl at thirty-eight . . . probably her last baby," said Kicho. "My husband would better have a few concubines than falling in love with Mrs Saucepan. She is too smart."

Kicho watched the ducks flying away from the surface of the lake.

Hiroko said, "I am forty-two and I don't think I would be able to have any more babies, but Hide . . ." She paused blushing.

"You are blessed with four children, Hiroko. I am barren," said thirty-seven year old Kicho. Hiroko opened her mouth trying to say something, but was unable to find a word of consolation.

In the following year, Mrs Saucepan, in her thirties, had a son by Nobunaga, who appropriately nicknamed him "Ladle".

*

In July 1572, Nobunaga called his second and third sons to Gifu Castle to perform an initiation at the same time with his heir. Kicho's adopted son Lord Strange said to her in private, "Why three of us in one ceremony? Am I not special? I am your adopted son and the heir."

"Your father was forced to fight against many to establish his status as the heir. After losing your grandfather at the age of sixteen, the succession right was not given to him. You are lucky to have your father's protection, but, I am sure he feels the need to train you as his heir. You need to prove yourself to him."

"I am afraid that he is unhappy with me. He allows Tea-whisk and Three-seven a lot more fun and freedom."

[47] Nobunaga nicknamed her Nabe, which means a saucepan

"He thinks you are special and you *are*. Tea-whisk and Three-seven only need to worry about their own districts. You need to worry about all Japan. Your task is harder, I think, than what your father faced when he was your age."

Kicho thought Lord Strange was her treasure. She had no way of foreseeing the tragedy to fall on him in ten years.

*

Kicho found various cultural activities in Kyoto and loved it. Nobunaga appreciated her associations with the academics through her brothers who were high priests in Kyoto. Hide also had associations with them as a cousin. Nobunaga had a ground breaking ceremony for construction of Kicho's residence at Mushakoji, Kyoto on March 24, 1572. The residence was situated at the north of the shogunate's palace. Nobunaga always avoided the troops coming into Kyoto, fearing their misbehaviour. He made a strict provision that no troops were to camp near the palace or Kicho's residence.[48] Nobunaga left Hide in charge of Kyoto politics and left Kicho to oversee him. Nobunaga travelled between Kyoto where Kicho lived and Gifu, her home.

Nobunaga and his ally Yasu's coalition lost the Battle of Mikatagahara against the Takedas. In December, 1572. The Shogun initiated the Oda Encircling Net of military warlords against Nobunaga in an attempt to crush him and regain the Ashikaga shogunate's political power. Unfortunately for the shogun, Takeda Shingen, the prominent warlord opposed to Nobunaga, died in April, 1573 and Nobunaga chased Shogun Ashikaga Yoshiaki away from Kyoto. In August, 1573, he conquered the Azais and the Asakuras.

Nobunaga asked him to become his retainer, but, Ichi's husband Azai Nagamasa, who fought against Nobunaga five times, refused and committed seppuku at Kotani Castle. Ichi and her daughters including Cha-cha returned to Kiyosu. Kicho did not allow Ichi to live at Gifu

---

48 This is on record. See the references of the Japanese version of Kicho & Nobunaga.

with Nobunaga, and neither of them protested. As with everyone else at Gifu Castle, they knew who had the best policy.

*

"I'll show you something," Nobunaga beamed at Kicho in the private lounge.

"It is a beautiful box. I wonder what treasure is inside."

Nobunaga watched Kicho, smiling.

Kicho sat in front of the large box and bowed according to the manners for appreciating an art work. She took off the lacquered lid adorned with gold inlays and put her hands inside. Lifting a large lacquered pot, her face turned pale and she dropped it.

"Be careful, Kicho."

"Is this who I think it is?"

"It is a skull, cured and lacquered with many layers.[49] It belonged to Azai Nagamasa. It is a prize head, my trophy. He betrayed me and we fought; we made amends and fought five times. I gave him Ichi. I wanted him to be my brother. He eventually chose death rather than to be my subordinate, but he did not murder-suicide with her. I am going to show everyone that there was no hatred between us. We shared a mutual respect."

Kicho heard afterwards that Nobunaga showed off the trophy to his major retainers at the New Year's party, and when Monkey admired it everyone followed suit. Kicho wondered if they were all trying to please their master. By this time, there weren't many who dared to disapprove of anything Nobunaga did.

*

By 1575, only eight years since he met Hide, Nobunaga had conquered most of the warlords to the north of Kyoto.

"I shall give Lord Strange Gifu Castle together with the districts of Owari and Mino to declare my retirement. To oversee the peace of

---

[49] Shincho Koki

the recently conquered districts, I shall build a castle on a hill by Lake Biwa, halfway between Kyoto and Gifu. The hill is called the Peace-Mound or Azchi."

Nobunaga started to construct the castle at the beginning of 1576. When the temporary residence at the foot of the hill was completed in February, in order to oversee the construction, he moved in with Mrs Saucepan. Mrs Saucepan was talented in music and literature. Shamisen[50] was heard often from her residence.

*

In early 1576, Nobunaga accompanied Kicho to stay at her brother's temple[51] in Nijo. They saw a neighbour's beautiful Japanese garden.

"It reminds me of Lord Viper's garden."

"My grandfather was a trainee priest at this Myokaku temple. He took the idea to Mino."

"There are hills, streams, ponds with colourful fish and cherry trees . . ."

"I've seen various gardens in Kyoto, but this one is very special. It makes me feel at home."

"We need a home in Kyoto, I'll get it for you."

"How lovely, my lord . . . but the house is run down . . ."

"We will have it refurbished, with a sauna[52] for you. I put Hide in charge for politics in Kyoto. You can stay here and make sure Hide does the right thing. You are the most suitable person for the role as you and Hide have many mutual friends and relatives."

Nobunaga started the refurbishment in April, 1576.

*

[50] a small guitar like instrument made of cat's skin.

[51] Lord Viper had asked Nobunaga to make Kicho's brothers priests.

[52] The have recently discovered sauna at the site. See Japanese version for details.

At this time, he ordered Hide to join Sakuma and attack the resisting priest soldiers at Mount Rock near Kyoto.[53] Nobunaga had kept Sakuma in charge for this holy temple in Osaka for five years, but there had been little progress. In May, Hide and Sakuma's coalition army was trapped within a circle of the priests' army. Nobunaga urged other warlords to join the rescue party, but it took them too long to arrive.

"I must save Hide at any cost."

Nobunaga jumped on his horse but only three thousand direct retainers followed him. Nobunaga was the target of his enemies. A young horseman on his right got shot and fell off the horse; a samurai on his left was shot and died instantly. In the fierce attack by the priests, Nobunaga was shot in the leg.[54] Bearing the pain, he put all his strength in his leg to hold on. He kept riding and finally reached the priest soldiers to break the ring.

Hide and Sakuma's men all cheered to see Nobunaga. Hide and Mino samurai were Nobunaga's relatives through Kicho. When most warlords under the shogun were against Nobunaga, Mino samurai and Hide had stood firmly by his side.

Hide continued to battle and negotiate with the priests. He returned to Hiroko at Sakamoto Castle in June.[55]

"You look terrible, please rest." Hiroko felt his fever. Hide stayed in bed for a few days when Nobunaga sent a famous doctor, Manase Dosan, who diagnosed his illness as tuberculosis.

Kicho and Nobunaga visited Hide at his bedside on June 26, 1576.[56] There was a rumour in town that Hide had gotten sick for disturbing the holy temple.

"The rumour has no grounds", Nobunaga assured him.

"You just obeyed my orders. If Mount Rock has any supernatural powers, its curse is on me, not you."

Kicho was alarmed to see Hiroko's haggard face.

"You'd better rest, Hiroko."

---

53 Ishiyama(Mount Rock) Hongan-temple at Osaka

54 Shincho Koki

55 This is where Osaka Castle stands today.

56 See Akechi Chronicle

"Lady Kicho is right, dear. You've had no rest for many days and nights, changing the cloth to cool my forehead . . ."

Younger women, including Kicho's sister who had married Hide's retainer, and Hide's sisters were there, but they were just chatting and giggling. Kicho scowled.

Hide was better by October, but by then Hiroko had became bedridden. Hide called professional prayers, but she grew weaker and passed away peacefully on November 22, 1576. Hide was by her bedside.

Did I work too hard to compete with Sakuma and Monkey trying to prove myself to Nobunaga? Hiroko was so proud of me when I became the first lord of the castle among all retainers, but my achievements are meaningless, now without her.

He had other regrets.

I was the shogun's direct retainer and had an ambition to control all Japan in his administration. Given the opportunity, I could have been the shogun myself as my Akechi clan has the Genji bloodline connecting to the shogun. Nobunaga has become a dictator, replacing the powers of shogun which should have belonged to the Genji bloodline . . . me, for example.

Kicho became concerned.

"Since his illness, Hide has become emotionally unstable. I think he needs a vacation."

"Lord Kototsugu from the Imperial Court complained that Hide took advantage of them. It is time I handled Kyoto myself."

"Lord Kototsugu is friendly with commoners. He will be a good ambassador."

The refurbishment of the new Nijo residence was completed in July and Nobunaga handled Kyoto politics through Lord Kototsugu.

Kicho had two younger brothers who were high priests in Kyoto. Her other brother included Shingoro, [57] Lord Strange's chief retainer, another brother was in Nobunaga's administration.[58] Kicho shared happy times with Nobunaga and she loved the cultural entertainment in Kyoto.

---

[57] Shingoro is believed to be Kicho's full brother.

[58] Toshiaki See Wikipedia

Nobunaga travelled between his three bases regularly. Mrs Saucepan stayed in Azchi and another concubine, Lord Strange's former nurse, was in Gifu. The Imperial Court appointed Nobunaga as the Prime Minister in November.

On New Year's Day 1578, Nobunaga invited his major retainers including Hide, Lord Strange and Monkey to a tea ceremony party at Azchi.[59] The seven storied Azchi Castle stood proudly by Lake Biwa. Kicho's lounge was furnished by fusuma with gold inlays and a Kano Eitoku painting of a mother pheasant grooming her chicks. Nobunaga moved to Azchi, but Kicho remained in Kyoto where she had many relatives and friends.

A few days after the tea party, there was a fire in the town of Azchi. Terraced homes made of wood and paper burnt easily. It was a criminal negligence which destroyed many neighbouring homes and lives.

When Nobunaga investigated the cause, it was found that the homes were unattended at the time of fire as the wives of the archery squad still lived in Mino and Owari.

"They have told their wives to come to Azchi, but the wives didn't listen because they are happier back home."

"If they can't make their wives come to Azchi, I will do it for them."

Nobunaga ordered the burning down of the homes of the archery squad and now homeless, the wives moved to Azchi.[60]

*

Monkey's wife Nene visited Nobunaga at Azchi Castle early in the summer of 1579.[61]

"I'll show you the tower, Nene." He led his way quickly climbing up the steep stairs.

"I am honoured."

"This is Kicho's lounge."

---

[59] Shincho Koki

[60] Shincho Koki

[61] http://en.wikipedia.org/wiki/Nene_(aristocrat) last accessed 24/9/11

Nene was out of breath. ". . . So, spacious, and luxurious, doesn't Lady Kicho live here?"

"She likes Kyoto too much."

"You are kind to her. I am envious."

"Doesn't Monkey look after you?"

"He has been taking many concubines in Kyoto."

"Has he?"

"He has even started to send love letters to women at the Court."

"Oh . . . No wonder you are concerned. But Nene, you grow more beautiful every time I see you. You are a too good a wife for Monkey. You look more beautiful now than when I first met you fifteen years ago."

"Please don't tease me, my lord." She was thirty-three and had taken special care with her make up to visit Nobunaga.

"No kidding. It's true. Don't worry, Nene, Monkey loves and appreciates you. I know it."

"Do you really think so, my lord?"

"Of course. Think about it, Nene. You *are* the wife. Don't waste time being jealous of concubines. Kicho doesn't. She has left me alone with Mrs Saucepan for a long time. Actually, I don't mind her to be a little jealous, sometimes."

Nene bowed blushing. "I'll try to follow our lady's example."

Nobunaga looked far beyond Lake Biwa towards Kyoto where Kicho lived. Nene stood behind him looking in the same direction. The breeze fluttered her long black hair.

"My husband and I have been married for twenty years and he has taken many concubines, but, I am afraid he is sterile . . ."

Nene breathed in and continued.

"I wonder whether . . . if there is any chance of you letting me adopt your fifth son Otsugimaru . . ."

"What . . . ?"

Nobunaga started to turn his neck to Nene.

If I gave her Otsugimaru, it will confirm her as Monkey*'s wife. Monkey then will not be able to take a wife from the Court to form political alliance.*

"I will write a letter for you telling Monkey to stop taking concubines, Nene." [62] He looked at Lake Biwa's mirror-like surface.

"How kind of you."[63] Nene bowed behind him.

"I will think about Otsugimaru as well," Nobunaga turned half way showing his handsome profile.

"If you are so kind to let me adopt Otsugimaru, I will cherish and protect him as long as I live."

I can count on an intelligent adopted mother like Nene, should Monkey have a son by a concubine later.

The breeze was pleasant at the top of Mount Azchi. Nene remembered something Nobunaga should know,

"Whenever I visit Lady Kicho's residence, Hide's pages are waiting outside."

"Really?" Nobunaga turned to stare at Nene for a moment. He quickly turned back to look towards Kyoto.

"I am glad Hide is doing his job. I placed him in charge of policing Kyoto."

Nene said nothing more.

**

In March, 1579, Lord Kototsugu of the Imperial Court died. Intelligent and friendly, he had been a good ambassador between the Court and Nobunaga. Other Court people talked in such roundabout ways, Nobunaga never had enough patience to negotiate with them.

It had been four years since Hiroko's death, but Hide did not take a wife or a concubine. In July 1579, Hide's mother, Lady Maki, sent a messenger to Kicho to say that Hide had returned from Yakami Castle. His troops had surrounded the castle for a year. Kicho and Kano decided to walk to Hide's residence which was also at Nijo.

"The cherry blossoms have nearly finished, but it is still nice to take a stroll."

---

[62] Nene must have treasured this letter and showed it off to many: It still exists. Wikipedia

[63] The letter still exists. Wikipedia

"Thanks to Lord Nobunaga, Kyoto is a safe place for women again."

"Lady Maki said that she will call a noh dancer for us."

"I always wanted to meet that famous actor."

Forty-four year old Kicho and forty-eight year old Kano giggled like teenage girls.

At Hide's residence, Lady Maki and Hide were looking serious.

"When we threw some food, the starving enemy soldiers flocked on it. We shot at one of them and he was eaten alive by the others."

"How awful."

"The soldiers revolted and captured the lords of the castle. They demand a relative of mine as surety in exchange."

"Your three daughters are married and you only have one son, your heir, at home. We cannot part with him, no way. He is asthmatic and it is too risky for him. Let *me* go, Hide."

"Mother . . ."

"I am seventy-three. I've lived long enough to see your wonderful achievements. I won't have many more years left and if I can save my grandson's life, I have no regrets at all."

"Mother, I am so indebted to you."

"Don't worry. It is an inconvenience for a short time. It is my pleasure to be useful for you at my age."

*

Kicho went to Azchi.

"Please my lord, spare the lives of the conceding lords of Yakami Castle to save Lady Maki's life."

"You never came to Azchi when I called. Did you come to ask me to spare your aunt's life?"

"Lady Maki is not just an aunt, she is almost like my mother."

"If the lords came to Azchi on their own accord in order to save their retainers, I would have spared their lives. They, however, waited too long and lost the respect of their retainers. Their lives are worth nothing now. Hide was stupid to send Lady Maki. There was no need for it because they have conceded."

Nobunaga executed the lords of Yakami Castle without delay and Lady Maki was executed by the enemies in revenge.

Kicho woke with a cold sweat in the night. She had a nightmare that Lady Maki was being eaten alive by the starving soldiers.

I could not save the life of someone who was dear to me. I don't know what to say to Hide. I wonder if he had the same nightmare.

Kicho remembered the time when she saved Lady Ohmi and sixteen women in Gifu.

I was able to do that because he loved me then, but now . . .

Kicho did not know that Nobunaga had always disliked Lady Maki and the feeling had been mutual. Kicho's mother and Lady Maki had both thought Hide was the suitable husband for Kicho. After the fall of Akechi Castle, Hide had declined Nobunaga's offer to be his retainer and went seeking work elsewhere. Lady Maki's relatives in the Asakura clan eventually found a position for Hide. The Asakuras, like the Azais, had believed that their heritage was superior to Lord Fool's.

*

It seemed that Nobunaga had become unreasonable tyrant since Lord Kototsugu's death. Nobunaga gave "permission" to commit suicide to his son-in-law, Toku's husband, who was suspected of betrayal.[64]

In a separate incident, Nobunaga captured and executed the families of unfaithful retainers, including Hide's grandchildren.[65] Kicho tried in vain to save her young relatives. Nobunaga burned the unfaithful retainers' servants alive in a locked house.[66]

Nobunaga's reputation deteriorated fast. When Nobunaga went to the Court, no one came to see him as they couldn't decide whose job it was to see the difficult man. Nobunaga lost patience and left. Even Nobunaga realised, then, that Hide was needed to come back to Kyoto politics.

---

[64] Shincho Koki

[65] Hide's daughter was married to Araki's son who betrayed Nobunaga with the father. She had returned earlier in the negotiation leaving the children behind.

[66] It refers to the Araki's servants.

Nobunaga gave their Nijo residence to the Court after its refurbishment. It was probably a part of the policy to rescue his reputation; or perhaps he had considered what Nene had said. Kicho had no option but to pack and go to Azchi.

Hide worked hard and he was a good negotiator. Priest soldiers vacated Mount Rock ending Nobunaga's eleven year long bloody battle with them. Nobunaga rewarded Hide's work, but it was at the expense of someone else. As soon as the priests were gone in August 1580, Nobunaga retrenched Sakuma who had been surrounding Mount Rock for him for ten years.

"Sakuma is lazy and useless, so, Hide shall have his property." Furthermore, Nobunaga said,

"Hayashi betrayed me twenty-three years ago, so I will dismiss him, as well."

Sakuma and Hayashi did not have capable successors and it became clear to everyone that Nobunaga did not approve an automatic right of inheritence. Sakuma and Hayashi who knew Nobunaga since childhood were often not afraid to talk back to Nobunaga. Kicho was afraid that Nobunaga became impatient to listen and became to value the retainers, such as Monkey, who blindly carried out his orders.

In the following January, 1581, Nobunaga built a horse training ground in Azchi. Forty-eight year old Nobunaga trained his horses from dawn till dusk, day after d*ay*, like an obsessed child.

How nice that he has found something that he loves. Kyoto politics was not for him after all. While I was concerned about Hide's depression, I had forgotten that my husband has also suffered from stress in the past years.

Since his injury to save Hide at Mount Rock, he has not been in a battle. He became cautious with the huge responsibility on his shoulders, the peace and security for the much wider distrusts of Japan. It must have been stressful for him, who is used to lead a pack in fierce battles, rather than to handle the people of Kyoto.

After a month of training, in February, Nobunaga exhibited a large scale horse show at Kyoto in front of the Emperor. The women of the Imperial Court were dressed beautifully, and thanks to Nobunaga, the citizens of Kyoto had the pleasure of seeing them.

There were horse parades and competitions by Nobunaga's festively dressed sons and major retainers. Nobunaga changed his horses and costumes several times. Each time, he rode like a "flying bird."[67] When he rode his *Big Black*,[68] Kicho thought she was seeing *Monokawa* who died at the Battle of Okehazama.

In those days, not a day passed without worrying about his life and safety, but thinking back, it was the happiest time of my life. I was in love. Everyone admires him now and he never doubts my love for him, but do I really love him?

*

Two weeks after the horse show in Kyoto, on March 10, 1581, the maids at Azchi Castle chatted,

"Lord Nobunaga and his pages have gone to see his fifth son Otsugimaru and adopted mother Lady Nene, while Lord Monkey is away at war."

"He is going to accompany Otsugimaru to visit Chikubu Island 7 km away from there."

"They are going to visit the temple on the island by boat."

"Lord Nobunaga's party rode horses to Nene's castle, which is 40 km away, so there and back including the boat ride will be close to 100 km. There is no way they will be back today."

"Lady Nene would be entertaining the lord, I guess."

"That means . . . a day off for us all!"

The maids cheered.

"The priest at nearby Kuwami Temple has invited us all to a lecture."

"It is an ideal day for a stroll."

Kicho joined the maids. As she climbed down Mount Azchi in her light weight zori, she thought a lot.

I wonder why my husband wore the ancient Chinese emperor's outfit at the horse show . . . Is it possible that he wants to be the emperor's relative as a

---

67 Shincho Koki

68 大黒

policy? If I become a nun, he will be free to remarry a woman of the Imperial Court. His reputation this year has improved and the beautifully dressed women of the Court adored him. I shouldn't be jealous as I am Nobunaga's wife, not a wife of an ordinary man. If I become a nun, I will be free from this womanly torment."

Kicho was forty-seven.

Azchi Castle was peaceful all day. The gatekeeper felt so relaxed in the afternoon sun that he could fall asleep. He thought he might sit down . . . if no one was watching . . . He looked around and rubbed his eyes.

What is that? A horse?

At the bottom of the hill, he saw several horses galloping through the straight and wide main street, where newly built houses stood on either side. The man leading the pack is . . .

He can't be.

The next moment, the gatekeeper yelled, "The lord is back!"

The gatekeeper hardly had time to organise a messenger before Nobunaga's horse stopped right in front of him.

"Where are the maids?"

"Gone? Where?"

"What? A day off without my permission?"

Nobunaga didn't get off the horse. He rode directly to Kuwami Temple and yelled.

"Where is Kicho? She is not going to be a nun."

He was enraged to see all the maids there.

"Do you run away if I don't tie you down with a rope?"

The maids feared for their lives. Nobunaga tied them up in one long line of rope, which was the way to march criminals to the site of their execution.[69]

Kicho returned on horseback. She was secretly amused by his rage.

Did he get upset because he thought I was going to be a nun?

---

[69] There have been records which said Nobunaga killed the priest and the maids who left work without permission, but, later it was found that the priest lived for his natural life. Wikipedia Japanese version.

*

In the middle of that night, Nobunaga came to Kicho. His seventeen year old page Ranmaru was running after his master as usual. Kicho was asleep.

Is he angry still? The last time he came to my bed, he could not do it and got angry. I do not need him losing his temper again.

Without a word, Nobunaga laid beside her.

Kicho sensed that he was not in the mood for a chat, so she gently put her arms around his neck. There was no reaction. She tentatively slid her hand down below. She closed her eyes in case she did not like his look. Nobunaga pushed her head down. Kicho opened her mouth. It moved a little in her mouth. She was relieved.

I was able to please him.

It kept growing, filling her mouth, and soon it became difficult for her to breathe.

Why do I have to do this? It is Mrs Saucepan's job. It tastes worse than before . . .

Nobunaga moaned.

He will come soon, I hope. Am I doing it right for him?

Nobunaga said, "Turn over."

Kicho was a little worried because his face, illuminated by the lantern, was not smiling, but she obeyed.

When he pulled up her kimono, the whiteness of her bottom floated in the dark. Nobunaga stretched his arm towards the lantern and skillfully took out the oil.

"No . . ."

Kicho tried to get away, but it was too late. Nobunaga put his weight on her thighs and she could not move.

An unbelievable pain made Kicho stop breathing.

She called, "Help . . . ," but there was no way that Ranmaru, waiting in the gallery, would come to her rescue. Kicho sobbed every time he moved, crushing the corner of the futon in her hands. In between the waves of pain, Kicho remembered Juami, who was killed by another retainer.

Did Juami bear pains like this since the age of twelve? Did he love the lord despite this?

I was a naive wife who never appreciated Juami's innocent love for Nobunaga. To love, for Juami was to endure . . . Nobunaga knew it and it was why he trusted him with me when he took all the other men to the battle. Juami endured knowing he pleased Nobunaga . . . and even after Nobunaga stopped calling him to his bed, he did not stop loving him . . . Is love to endure? Should I, a wife endure?

As she thought of Juami, the pain eased and strangely became pleasurable. A little later, when it became painful again, Nobunaga groaned and he was done. They did not move for a long time. There was no sound in the gallery where Ranmaru waited.

*

Kicho heard the sparrows and opened her eyes. The morning sun was coming through the gaps of the fusuma sliding doors. She was pleasantly surprised to find Nobunaga beside her. He looked relaxed. How many years has it been since . . . ? She remembered how nice it was to feel his skin.

"I am sorry . . . to hurt you."

"I was . . . I am happy to see you, like this."

"I have forgiven the maids and let them free."

"Thank you . . . I missed you . . ." Kicho snuggled up to Nobunaga and he wrapped Kicho's hands with his. Kicho wanted to cry.

"I was impressed with Nene being in charge and taking the security of the castle seriously while Monkey was away at war. I returned early because something told me to . . . and I am glad I did."

"You went so far away with only a few body guards. Did you think *you* were safe?"

"Lord Fool is allowed to do what he wants. I know whether I am safe or not; but when you are not with me, I worry. Kuwami Temple has a deep moat like a castle. A villain can take you as a hostage."

"Take me wherever you go, then, my lord."

"Good. Lord Strange has become capable of handling the physical battles. You and I can work on the Imperial Court. Hide's way will take a hundred years. A man's life is fifty years . . . I've only got one more year."

"Don't you dare . . . Remember, you told the farmers that they can live to eighty, if they worshiped you!"

"Ha, ha. I love your idea of admission fees to see inside Azchi Castle and donations to worship me for a long life."

"That is what the temples do . . ."

"You learned the system from your high priest brothers, right?"

When they laughed together, Kicho felt happiness.

*

Nobunaga had a summer festival on July 15, 1581. The boats on the lake, the path to the top of Mount Azchi and the castle tower were all illuminated by numerous torches. The people gathered from far away to see the spectacular sight.

Kicho remembered the Tsushima Shrine summer festival she went to with Nobunaga every year when they were at Kiyosu Castle.

We watched the boats carrying torches from the humble makeshift viewing platform, mingling with village commoners . . . it was the happiest moment of my life . . .

*

In the following March, 1582, Lord Nobunaga gave Lord Strange a crafted sword and said, "You are the military head of all Japan."

He then rewarded Yasu with two more districts. Yasu, who lost his disgraced heir with Nobunaga's "permission"[70] to commit suicide had remained Nobunaga's faithful ally. Yasu had constructed new roads and bridges for Nobunaga's journey which impressed Nobunaga.

Kicho had told Nobunaga that she was worried that Yasu had hard feelings about Nobunaga's controversial "permission" for his heir's

---

[70] Earlier documents stated Nobunaga "ordered" him, but recent findings indicate that he only gave "permission". See Wikipedia (Japanese version.)

seppuku. Nobunaga wanted to let her know that she didn't need to worry.

She is always worried about what others think of me!

Nobunaga decided to cut the journey short and go back to Kyoto earlier than scheduled. When he galloped on *Big Black*, there were not many who could keep up. Only Ranmaru and a few others with determined eyes chased after him along the path through the green forests leading to Kyoto.

*

Kicho was waiting for Nobunaga at a house within the Myokaku Temple where her brother was a high priest. Hide visited knowing that Nobunaga was still a few days away.

". . . He killed my mother."

"That is not true. It was your decision to send her as a surety knowing the risk, Hide."

Hide lowered his voice, although the maids had been dismissed for privacy.

"My innocent grandchildren were executed, too. Don't you think that he has become a tyrant in recent years?"

"I am really sorry for what happened to your grandchildren, but please remember that my husband negotiated for one whole year with the Arakis, prior to his desparate decision."

In the past several years, Hide had suffered a serious illness. He lost his wife, his mother and grandchildren all in tragic circumstances. Further, he had lost his sister in August of the previous year through tuberculosis, which was reminiscent of Hiroko's death and the depression he had suffered following her death.

Kicho became the only person with whom Hide could confide. He would normally be satisfied to be listened to, but this day he shook his head.

"It took Nobunaga eleven long years to move to Mino after he received the bequest from Lord Viper. Once he met me, it took him only a month to re-establish the new government with the shogun. Even he admitted that Owari samurai have been useless. That's why he dismissed

Hayashi and Sakuma. We Mino samurai have done much of the work uniting Japan. We have been used. You too, my lady."

Kicho looked at Hide through the draping net which separated them.

Why is he so aggressive, today?

"I don't wish to hear this anymore." She covered her ears with hands and shook her head.

"Please go now."

"No, Kicho . . ."

"You are rude to call me Kicho. I am your lord's wife."

"I am sorry, my lady. Please forgive me."

Hide put his hands on the tatami and started to push himself backwards, then his hands stopped. His eyes glittered.

The lady in front of him was the tyrant's wife who defended her husband, but she was also, as Hide knew, just a woman. Many years ago, Hide had shown her the way of love. He might have regretted giving her away to Nobunaga. Was it desire or lust to conquer? Fifty-five year old Hide, who had not had a woman since he lost his wife five years ago, found the feeling growing within him unbearable.

Kano had been sent away and no sound came from the gallery where she waited. When Hide put his hand to the draping net, Kicho knew what was to happen.

Was she afraid for it to happen for a long time, or was she waiting for it? Either way, she had not forgotten the pleasure and pain . . .

"Please, don't." She begged twice.

The birds outside fluttered their feathers, chasing.

The draping net moved a little at first and gradually more. Like the rippling waves coming and receding, Kicho's sighs became sniffles and then sobs. Hide asked, "All right?"

When Hide came out, he was dressed immaculately, the same as when he came.

Beyond the drapes, Kicho sat with her hair messy, the front of her Kimono undone. Her robe was thrown to the floor. She had her palm on her mouth. She was beside herself.

I never felt as deeply with my husband. I am glad that I lived to this day. Showered by relentless praise, I forgot who I was. He said he never stopped loving me, even when he was married to Hiroko and I willingly believe . . .

*

There were noises of greetings from the entrance hall as Hide farewelled Kicho's servants. When he and his followers were gone, it was quiet again. Then, the sound of horses galloping approached fast. The horses stopped in front of the house.

Almost as soon as Kano called, "The lord is back," Nobunaga stood in Kicho's room.

"Are you ill?"

He put a hand on the drape and stopped. He eyes were on Kicho's robe on the floor.

"I smell rotten fish."

He came through, then turned white.

He pushed her to the floor, dividing the hem of her kimono, he thrust his hand inside. He then rubbed his fingers and put them to his nose.

"Hide went home just then, I heard." His voice was husky. "Is it true?"

He glared at her. "Tell me."

As he waited, his shoulders swayed.

Kicho sat hanging her head down. She did not move, did not even attempt to tidy her hair or the front of her kimono.

"Please, my lord, punish me by death."

Sparrows chirped outside.

"I don't wish to live any longer, so, please, go ahead and punish me."

"Good."

She sat with both hands on the tatami. Nobunaga pulled out his sword. The blade caught the light in the shadow of the drapes. It was the famous sword that he won at the Battle of Okehazama.[71] It had

---

[71] Yoshimoto Samonji, which was a wedding gift from the Takedas to the Imagawas when Takeda Shingen's elder sister married Imagawa

proven its quality many times since; Kicho had seen an example at the construction site of Nijo Castle.

No doubt that it would be a quick painless death. Nobunaga lifted the sword and the drape moved a little. The birds were still fluttering feathers outside.

Nobunaga held the sword high, but he could not move. Kicho, picked up an embroidered case which had dropped on the tatami and pulled out her dagger. It was the engagement present from Lord Viper. Did she forget his words, never to commit suicide?

As she held the tip of the blade against her throat, Nobunaga flicked her hands with a foot. Throwing his sword behind him, he stood on Kicho's dagger. He then grabbed her shoulders.

"Were you raped?

She was silent.

"If he raped you, he shall die."

Kicho shook her head side to side, slowly looking up. Her eyes welled.

"If you consented he shall live. Tell me which."

Kicho moved her head in the same way as before. Did she understand what was asked?

Nobunaga took his hands off her and looked to his side.

"Do you love him?"

"I love only you."

"Liar. Did you think I didn't know about you and Hide before you came to Owari?"

"There was nothing between us. Believe me. I made a mistake today. I only love you. It is true."

Nobunaga kicked her. He kicked again and again. He glared at her as his tears fell.

Kicho sat on tatami as she was kicked. Strangely, it did not hurt. She remembered Nobunaga had kicked Hirate repeatedly before Hirate committed seppuku.[72]

"Please, my lord, punish me by death."

Yoshimoto.

[72] Form of suicide by cutting own belly.

"Good."

Nobunaga picked up the sword from the tatami.

Kicho put her long hair to one side, loosened the collar of her dishevelled kimono to expose her white neck and waited for his sword to come down. She remembered the time she went to see the Portuguese missionary at the construction site of Nijo Castle. Like the head of the young offender, Kicho's head would roll. Fresh blood would ooze out of the cut in the neck.

When it was decided that she was to die, she remembered the carefree childhood days. She came to Owari, she fell in love and worried about Nobunaga's life being threatened. She remembered the sadness caused by Father and Brother Yoshi's fallout, followed by Father's tragic death: the torment she faced having to choose between Nobunaga and Brother Yoshi. She had tried hard to be a good wife . . . Happy memories and sad memories, everything that happened in her life flashed like a revolving lantern.

Now it was decided that she was to be executed by her husband, strangely, she did not feel guilty about Hide. It was just one of many memories, a rather nice one.

With a sound of the sword slicing the air, Nobunaga swayed the blade down. When she closed her eyes, she saw her head roll. She peed, though she did not know.

She saw Juami kowtowing flat on the kitchen floor begging Nobunaga's forgiveness for fondling Nene.

Juami's tears on his eyelashes represented his anguish towards Nobunaga's selfish outrage, for Juami showing interest in someone else after Nobunaga stopped calling him to his bed . . . Juami didn't want to talk about it with me, then, and I didn't know why, but now I understand. How could he, I was Nobunaga's wife. His rival. I understand the meaning of his tears now because I am in the same position as he was . . . I shall see dear Juami soon in another world . . .

With the sound of the sword clicking back in the case, Kicho came back to her senses.

Why am I not hurting?

"Forgiven." Nobunaga stood crushing his hakama with both hands.

"I lived my life forgiving many who tried to kill me. Brother Katsu, Hayashi, Shibata . . . If I include their followers and retainers, I've forgiven thousands. I had forgiven Azai Nagamasa five times until he committed seppuku at the final time. You . . . never tried to kill me."

Nobunaga bit his lips and looked aside.

"What you've done is nothing."

His shoulders moved up, then down.

"I made you live in Kyoto to keep an eye on Hide. I can't blame you for doing what I asked."

"My lord . . ."

"Say nothing to Hide, understood?"

"Nothing?"

"He is also forgiven. I need him. I've given away two sisters,[73] two daughters,[74] four sons.[75] It was all for unity in Japan to end the civil war that I've given away my loved ones."

You love me?

"You are Nobunaga's wife, not a wife of an ordinary man. You have an important job to do."

"A job?"

"What do you think will happen to the order of Hide's troops and Lord Strange's troops with many Mino samurai? If you and I fall out, what do all the foot soldiers in Mino and Owari think of me? If I kill you, what would the men you brought up—Lord Strange and Shingoro or the samurai that married your sisters—think of me? We have only one more step to unify Japan, I can't afford to act emotionally."

When she heard this, Kicho wailed.

I just want to be loved as a woman. I don't care about unity in Japan, any more.

Ranmaru sat outside the gallery crushing his hakama with both hands.

**

---

[73] Refers to Inu and Ichi

[74] Refers to Toku and Fuyuhime

[75] Lord Tea-whisk, Lord Three-seven, Otsugimaru and Katsunaga See Wikipedia (Japanese) accessed 29.9.11.

Nobunaga invited Yasu in return and Yasu arrived in Azchi on May 15, 1582. Hide had the honour, as usual, of being the samurai in charge of entertaining Yasu. Hide was relieved to think that Nobunaga knew nothing about Kicho and him. He was a little worried when he heard that Nobunaga had returned earlier than anticipated.

Hide took great care, as he always did, in selecting the best ingredients for the menu. Delicacies included fermented fish from Lake Biwa.

Nobunaga sniffed, even before the dish was brought in.

"I smell rotten fish, Kumquat Head," said he, calling Hide by the citrus nickname he invented recently.

Hide replied, "The fermented fish has a unique aroma but is not rotten. It is a famous dish we have presented to the Imperial Court."

Nobunaga twitched his lips.

Yasu was gracious.

"Utterly delicious."

"Isn't it? It is Lady Kicho's favourite," said Hide unwittingly, and wiped the perspiration off his receding forehead not unlike a kumquat.

After lunch, Nobunaga called Hide for a meeting.

"Give two districts to the Chosokabe clan in Shikoku and make them submit."

"You have promised the Chosokabes all Shikoku, did you forget, my lord? Please don't change your policy and embarrass me."

"Embarrass you? What are you talking about, Kumquat Head? You embarrassed *me* in front of the guest at lunch." Nobunaga's face was red from consuming sake which he had not had since Hirate's death.

Just then, a messenger from Monkey arrived.

"The Mohris have called three assisting armies totaling half a million men. Monkey asks the lord to come to the rescue."

When he heard this, Nobunaga felt his blood boil. He had not had a good battle since talented warlords Takeda Shingen and Uesugi Kenshin had died. He had no time for the rotten fish.

"This is an opportunity not to be missed. I will go myself and conquer all the Chugoku districts and invade into Kyushu in one assault."

Nobunaga could see the final stage of uniting all Japan in front of him. He stood up overwhelmed.

"Kumquat Head, I will take your current districts off you. You shall go and conquer the districts of Izumo and Ishimi and make them yours instead."

Hide was still worried about the fish.

"Please don't punish me, my lord. Izumo and Ishimi both belong to Mohri,[76] the enemy."

"That is why I am telling you to go and conquer them. Don't you understand?"

"I beg you to reconsider. The districts of Izumo and Ishimi are far from Kyoto. You know that I am indispensable to Kyoto politics. Please keep me where I am." Hide did not know that Nobunaga wanted to separate him from Kicho.

"Kumquat Head!"

Nobunaga kicked Hide and Hide tumbled over to push and dislodge the fusuma partition with Kano Eitoku's sumie[77] painting completed only in the previous week. Luckily the fusuma, made of quality Mino paper, did not tear and Ranmaru's younger brothers Rikimaru and Bomaru placed it back. It was, however, not before Luis Frois, who was having lunch in the adjoining room, witnessed Ranmaru bash Hide's head, at his master's command.

Frois wrote that Nobunaga's behaviour was typical of a tyrant, but did he see blood on Ranmaru's white ceremonial fan? How did Hide feel?

Monkey kept sending messengers daily, sometimes twice daily with fresh news while Nobunaga was anxious to make any amends feeling indebted to Yasu for showing unchanged friendship. Nobunaga had no time to relax with Mrs Saucepan's silly parties for days. He used to enjoy surveying his territory on horseback daily in Owari and Gifu, but, at recently conquered Azchi, the routine was too dangerous.

---

76 (毛利) is pronounced Mohri with a long "o". The author adopted this spelling to distinguish this from a similar surname Mori, (森) as in Mori Ranmaru.

77 Paintings done by skilful strokes of brush in black ink

Ironically, Kumquat Head looked like Hirate, who committed seppuku after being repeatedly kicked by Lord Fool. Just as Lord Fool trusted Hirate's good nature, Prime Minister Nobunaga indulged in Kumquat Head's perseverance: so much so, he called him by his nickname in front of the other retainers. Everyone including Hide knew that Nobunaga had treated him exceptionally well as a relative. What Hide didn't know was that Nobunaga had also forgiven Hide's unforgivable misbehaviour. Hide would deserve more than a few bashings for Nobunaga to get even, wouldn't he?

On May 17, Nobunaga finished with Monkey's messengers at last. He dismissed Hide from entertaining, to prepare his troops for the battle. Hide had the honourable role, as expected, as the first retainer to lead an army to the battlefield.

After Hide left, Nobunaga went to the oval. Yelling and screaming, forty-nine year old Nobunaga raced one horse after another. When he was on *Big Black*, he looked like the same Lord Fool that had galloped Monokawa down the valley of Okehazama twenty-two years ago. His ambition to unite all Japan was near.

Hide had recommended a famous noh[78] actor to entertain Yasu on May 20. On the morning of May 19, impatient Nobunaga suddenly sent a messenger and ordered him to perform on the day.[79] The noh actor, Umewaka, hastily gathered costumes and instruments. Because they had no time to wait for a koshi, Umewaka and his accompanists climbed up the hill of Mount Azchi carrying a large furoshiki[80] full of goods.

Umewaka had been warned by Hide that Nobunaga would not allow a mistake. While he danced nervously, Umewaka perspired in his palms and dropped his dancing fan.

Nobunaga stood up angrily. His face was red from sake which he rarely consumed. Kicho would normally have held Nobunaga's sleeve to limit his sake, but, after her misbehaviour with Hide, she had reservations. Umewaka stopped the act and kowtowed and Nobunaga kicked him in front of the guest.

---

78 Slow moving traditional Japanese dance. Perhaps, not Nobunaga's taste.

79 Shincho Koki

80 Large peace of cloth used to wrap kimonos and goods for carrying.

Umewaka later went to see Hide to apologize.

"I am very sorry to let you down."

"Was he that mad?"

"My head was to be slashed off, I am sure, if it was not for the lady. She threw herself over me and begged the lord to kill her first."

"She didn't?"

"The lord calmed down later and let me play noh again. He then gave me ten sheets of gold, saying he did so only because the lady was afraid that people might think he got angry trying to save money. I know I don't deserve these. Please give them back to the lord."

"I can't."

"Then, please keep them yourself and I beg you never to recommend me to him. His face was as red as a cooked octopus. I have never seen anyone as mad as he."

Umewaka refused to take the gold sheets back and went home still shaking.

Why is he so easily upset recently? Why did Ranmaru show no mercy the other day?

He cursed at the gold sheets. He then moved his eyes to the green hydrangea flowers in the courtyard and kept staring at them. He covered his face and groaned.

*

The pages sat along the gallery outside Kumquat's lounge, facing the courtyard full of hydrangea. He held a secret meeting inside.

"Too risky, my lord." Akechi Hidemitsu whispered. He had succeeded the surname by marrying Kumquat's daughter who was divorced by the Arakis when they rebelled. She had endured the heartache of leaving two young children and moreover, they were executed when Araki escaped from his castle deserting them. Kumquat felt disappointed that his son-in-law did not express any hatred against Nobunaga.

"I am forced to do hard renegotiation with my relatives in Shikoku," considered Saito Rizo, whose sister-in-law had married a Chosokabe, the most domineering clan in Shikoku. ". . . but, at the time of the lord's power ever increasing, I will have to endure this."

"Our soldiers are supplied by Lord Nobunaga. Even if we succeed with the coup, it is hard to know what happens afterwords," said Kumquat's uncle, Akechi Mitsutada.

"Shibata, Monkey and Yasu will not automatically become your subordinates after the assassination, my lord," worried Fujita, a trusted retainer.

"Lord Nobunaga has been generous. We are proud of our achievements under him. Why should we take a risk?" said Akechi Hidemitsu, whom Kumquat relied on more than his own fifteen year old asthmatic son. Everyone agreed.

Kumquat asked, "Have you thought about what happened to Hayashi and Sakuma?"

"Hayashi-san tried many times to murder the lord until twenty-three years ago, while Sakuma-san was indeed useless. Lord Nobunaga was kind enough to give you Sakuma-san's former territory. Why are you concerned?"

Kumquat questioned,

"Don't you think he has become a mad dictator while we Mino's samurai did all the hard work for him? Isn't it unfair to take our current districts away in exchange for two districts still in the enemy's land?"

"I assure you, my lord, it is an expression Lord Nobunaga uses to motivate us. I don't doubt we will succeed in this expedition. Two new districts will be a challenge, I know, but, Lord Nobunaga himself has moved his headquarters four times. I don't believe he is giving this challenge to us out of hatred."

Kumquat wanted to scream,

Lady Kicho does not love her demented husband any more. She loves me!

Instead, he said,

"Lord Nobunaga will come to stay at Honno Temple with only twenty or so retainers, while I am ordered to lead 13,000 armed men and head in that direction. I just remembered Lord Viper's words that it is not a crime to take an advantage of an opportunity."

"I have heard of that, my lord, but . . ."

Hide urged, "It is the utmost rule in the time of upheaval. Lord Nobunaga himself destroyed his superiors, the Shibas and the shogun, to climb to the top. Why can't I do the same?"

"Lord Nobunaga never killed his superiors, my lord. He just took the political powers off them. That is the difference."

". . . All right I concede. You can all forget what I said."

*

After his retainers were gone, Hide held his head in both hands.

How can I convince them? Should I tell them about the lady and I? No, I can't disgrace her. Is there another way?

Hide glared at the hydrangea in the vase which had turned purple.

On May 26, Hide left his Sakamoto Castle near Kyoto.

If successful, I will live at Azchi. If not, I will die. Either way, I won't be back.

A duck swam on the surface of Lake Biwa followed by its ducklings and rippling waves. Hide looked up at the castle where he had spent happy days with his mother, wife and children. The cloud floating in the sky looked like the concerned face of Hiroko and then changed to the grave face of Lady Maki.

On May 27, Hide climbed Mount Atago to pray for a win. He bought fortune telling messages[81] written on small pieces of white paper three times, and three times he tied the messages on tree branches. Each said, "good luck."

It rained during the night. The next day, on May 28, Hide invited eight academics from Kyoto to a poetry making party. "Now is the time of rain fall in May," he wrote on the appropriate piece of stiff paper adorned with gold dust.

The leading poet and academic Satomura read this aloud and turned white. "The time" as homonym indicated Hide's heritage as "rain fall" did "to govern". Satomura closed his eyes. If he protested, he feared, his

81 They are called omikuji.

neck will be slashed. He took the brush pen with trembling fingers and dubbed black ink. He wrote,

"Falling flowers will stop the stream."

Did he mean to warn the risk or glorify the sacrifice?

Either way, Hide believed that the academics shared his view that Nobunaga was going ahead too fast.

On June 1, 1582, Hide called the same trusted retainers and confided in them about the poetry party. No one opposed, this time. Hide had been a good master. As the scheme was in public domain, live or die, they decided to follow their master's fate. No one was going to inform Nobunaga.

*

Nobunaga was relaxing at Honno Temple with Kicho and Lord Strange, after a stressful day seeing the prominent people of Kyoto.

"Father, you only have thirty immediate retainers guarding you tonight. Don't you think you are taking a risk? Even I have three thousand armed guards at Myokaku Temple. Should I send them over here to you tonight?"

"I have declared my retirement and introduced you to the people as the head of the Oda military force. It makes sense that you have more guards than me."

Lord Strange went back to Myokaku Temple where his concubine and their son slept peacefully.

*

On June 2, 1582 at dawn, Nobunaga woke with a noise in a distance. It sounded like soldiers quarrelling.

"Go and quiet them down, Ranmaru," he said.

Ranmaru's brother Bomaru answered.

"Ranmaru has already gone, my lord."

Bomaru heard his brother yell as he came running back. Something was awfully wrong.

"Rebellion! . . . It is a rebellion!"

"Rebellion? By whom?"

Nobunaga thought of Lord Strange, who had offered to send his troops. He thought of Lord Viper and Takeda Shingen who had been killed or chased away by their own sons.

Did he turn on me? I have brought him up strictly. I didn't allow my retainers' sons to automatically inherit their fathers' positions and I imposed the same burden on my son. If I made him chase the Takedas too hard, I was trying to educate him to be the ruler.

"I saw the crest of bellflower," Ranmaru cried.

"It can't be Hide . . ."

Kicho stood, tidying her breast layers of white night robe kimono. "Why Hide?"

"Hide never makes a mistake. He must have thought it through. There will be no escape from this."

Nobunaga pulled the string of his archery bow and a man in a shadow in distance fell with a scream. The arrows from the enemies kept coming straight at Nobunaga. After releasing a few more arrows, an arrow struck his elbow.

Bullets were hitting fusumas and the pillars like hail stones. When he turned, another arrow struck his back. He retreated to the hall of the temple, but all his men including Ranmaru's younger brother, twelve year old Bomaru, were outside trying to fend off the enemies. The enemies were all after Nobunaga.

Kicho tried to pull the arrow out of his back, but it was deep. If she forced it, she would pull the flesh with it. It must be cut at the stem.

She took out her pocket dagger given by Lord Viper as an engagement present.

I am going to use this against my throat, soon.

Nobunaga must have sensed her thought. He said,

"You get out, Hide will be kind to you," said he, as he pulled the arrow out himself.

"Uh . . ."

His white night robe kimono turned crimson at his back and blood kept spewing.

"Let me die with you. I introduced Hide thinking he will be good for you. I had no idea he would do this."

"It is not your fault. I forgot that he was Lord Viper's favourite. He had the same ambition . . . to rule all Japan."

Blood streamed from the corner of his mouth.

"I am not going to Hide. Let me die with you, my lord."

Ranmaru and Rikimaru, both with spatters of blood on them, were fending off the intruders. Kicho looked for the twelve year old Bomaru, but couldn't see.

"You should live. Hurry."

"Let me go to another world with you."

"You can't."

"Don't be so cruel to me, please. I am your wife."

"There is no other world. A person dies and that is it."

"My lord . . ."

"A dead man needs no wife. He lives only in people's memories. Azai Nagamasa let Ichi live, I shall let you live. After my death, there will be upheaval again. Live for Lord Strange and Hide to unite Japan."

Nobunaga held Kicho's shoulders in both arms and pushed her outside. Kicho saw Bomaru on the ground, lifeless.

"Hurry," said Nobunaga and ordered maids to take her out. Kicho turned back, but Nobunaga was faster. He ran into a room at the back of the hall, where spot fires had started. He slid the door shut in front of her.

With a sound of explosion, the flames escaped out of the room between the gaps of the sliding door. Kicho tried to run after him, but the maids held her tight. She was then caught by Hide's retainers, who pushed her away from the burning hall.

With another explosion, the main hall of the temple, where she came out seconds ago, was flooded with fire. Several explosions followed. Was there storage for the bombs?

My lord put fire on it and committed . . . , Alone.

The flames were reaching up to the sky which was becoming brighter. The fire caused the wind.

A scream echoed near the hall as someone called, "I got Ranmaru!"

His brothers won't be alive now,

Kicho closed her eyes and saw their mother's face.

Soldiers called,

"Look for Lord Nobunaga's body."

"The flame is too strong."

"Put out the fire."

"Water, fetch the water, from the dam, quickly!"

"Where is the body? Retrieve the head before it burns."

He won't be alive now. Tears fell out of both her eyes.

I won't be able to see him again. I won't be able to hear his voice . . . I hear Hide's voice somewhere. I don't want to see him . . . Never. If I am having a nightmare, I need to wake. I smell human flesh burning in the wind . . .

"Lady Kicho?" One of Hide's pages approached. Smeared with tears and cinder, she probably did not look like Nobunaga's lady. He took her to Hide.

Hide jumped off the horse.

"I have a koshi ready for you, my lady."

"I am not going to get into your koshi."

Hide looked puzzled.

"I shall take you to Azchi, my lady."

"I am not going with you . . . The lord had trusted you more than anyone else, more than his own son."

"No . . ."

"You were the only one whom he trusted with 13,000 armed men when he was unarmed."

"He was careless and it was my opportunity."

Kicho looked away as she too remembered Lord Viper's words, not to hesitate to take advantage of anyone including himself.

"I am asking Lord Strange to concede," Hide explained.

"Concede? Hardly possible. Lord Strange adores his father."

I am sure he will escape. I am not going to get into Hide's koshi and become his hostage.

"Give me a horse, please, Hide."

"If you insist."

Hide had the saddest face she had ever seen, but she did not care. Soldiers were still yelling at each other trying to find Nobunaga's body.

I hope they never find him. Hide does not deserve a trophy to prove that he conquered my husband.

Kicho turned the horse. A familiar looking samurai came after her on horseback.

"Please, my lady, let me accompany you to Azchi. It is too dangerous."

He was one of Kano's younger brothers, though Kicho could not remember his name. He offered her a man's riding jacket. Takeda Shingen and other warlords had let their soldiers rape the women and sold them to brothels but Hide's troops were well behaved.

My lord knew he could trust Hide with me . . .

Kicho felt Nobunaga's kindness, moments before his death. She looked for Kano, but she couldn't find her. Kicho and Kano's brother left Honno Temple on horseback.

There were scary moments with villains on the way. Kano's brother hired a boat across Lake Biwa overnight. He watched the captain all night holding his sword, until they reached the shore. They arrived at Azchi the next morning.

Kicho tumbled off the horse at the top of Mount Azchi.

"My lady! You are safe."

Gamou rushed out of the castle to meet Kicho. Nobunaga had left him as caretaker as he lived at his Hino Castle near Azchi.

"Lord Strange is dead?"

"He rushed to Honno Temple, but it was too late. He went to Nijo Castle to defend himself, but he eventually, committed seppuku. Your brother Shingoro followed him."[82]

"No . . ." Kicho sank down to the ground. She had hoped Lord Strange and Shingoro would escape.

Kano's brother had disappeared before she had a chance to thank him.

Little wonder. If caught, he will be slashed. I wonder where Kano has gone?

Toku met Kicho inside.

---

[82] Shincho Koki

"Mother, I heard that the lord's grandson, Lord Strange's heir is safe. Hide let them go free."

Nobunaga's mother, Lady Dota was calm. "Why are you wearing the Akechi's jacket?"

Kicho looked at the men's riding jacket she had been wearing. It had a small crest at her back, the Akechi's bellflower.

Gamou said, "Hide will be here soon with his army. It is too difficult to defend a large castle such as this with limited men. Lord Nobunaga's immediate retainers died at Honno Temple and Nijo Castle, and others are scattered in other parts of Japan. Please come to my Hino Castle. I will protect you there."

"Before we go, we should put fire to Azchi Castle," said Kicho. Toku and Lady Dota agreed.

"No," said Gamou. "It is a castle Lord Nobunaga took so much care to build."

"We should at least take the treasures with us, then," said Kicho; but Gamou disagreed, "I don't want to be a thief."

He was my retainer yesterday. The role has reversed overnight. The Gamous are generations of a prestigious family who had conceded to Nobunaga's military force. Gamou must be trying to take a mutual stand. Hide would be less likely to come after him if we left all the treasures.

Nobunaga's mother Lady Dota was a frail old lady, but, she started to select her clothes.

Her attitude does not compare to the time when Katsu died. Was Nobunaga the unloved son to the end?

Kicho moved four times with Nobunaga, to a more spacious and luxurious castle each time. She was then going to a much smaller castle, which did not belong to her. She burned all the personal letters including the ones she received from Nobunaga from the battlefields.

He said, 'Go to Hide.' I should have stayed with Hide. Hide at least is my relative. The Oda household without my husband is someone else's place.

She held her hand mirror with the bellflower design. She placed it between the layers of kimono in the crate made of woven bamboo.

A few days later at Hino Castle, Gamou brought news.

"On June 8, Hide vacated Azchi and receded to his Sakamoto Castle. Most of the samurai became Monkey's subordinates when he declared revenge."

"Revenge? How could he? Monkey said he needed to be rescued by my lord."

"Monkey captured Hide's messenger to the Mohris and made peace before they learned of the lord's death."

"What? . . . and now he is the samurai in charge for the revenge against Hide? Monkey must be looking to rule all of Japan."

Lord Strange used to get on well with Hide. Much better than with Monkey. If I had stayed with Hide as his hostage and helped him to make Lord Strange concede, all Mino samurai would have stayed with them. I have let down my husband. I could not protect Lord Strange and in effect helped Monkey benefit . . .

Kicho wept.

*

They never found Nobunaga's body.

After the fire subdued, they found the bodies of Ranmaru, Rikimaru and Bomaru. Among many other men, there was one woman's body—it was Kano holding her own dagger.

Lord Strange and Lord Tea-whisk were born only nine months apart. Kicho had refused until then to contemplate that it was impossible for one woman to give two births so close to each other.

When Kano fell pregnant, she had said to Nobunaga,

"Let me remain the lady's trusted maid."

"I will send Kitsuno home at the same time you take leave."

Baby Lord Strange came to Kiyosu Castle with a wet nurse and was adopted by Kicho. Kano returned separately. It was considered to be kinder for the barren Kicho.

Kano's brother later took some of his sister's hair home.

There stands a grave stone at Fudo-town, Gifu-city, today. The engraved message claims that it belongs to Nobunaga's wife, who died with her husband at Honno Temple. This led people to believe that Kicho died at Honno Temple, until recently.

Kano *devoted her life to me, but it was only while I was Nobunaga's wife. She did not want to spend the rest of her life as my friend . . .* *

Kicho never again saw Hide, who died eleven days after Nobunaga, from a stab wound inflicted by a highway robber while running away from Monkey's troops. Monkey staged a large-scale funeral for Nobunaga. He begged everyone from the Oda household to attend, but only Mrs Saucepan and Lady Dota obliged. None of Nobunaga's sons attended except for Otsugimaru who was Nene and Monkey's adopted son.

Kicho became a nun. A record at Myoshin Temple in Kyoto states that Kicho had an anniversary ceremony to commemorate Nobunaga's passing on June 2, 1583. This was held separately from the ceremony Monkey had in the name of Mrs Saucepan, who became Monkey's concubine's maid to earn her living.

Kicho did not need Monkey' favour as she had her own properties, and also, her adopted sons gave her money.[83] They urged her participation in politics as Nene did, but Kicho kept a low profile.

I did not know it when he was alive, but I had never cared about unification of Japan. I only wanted to be loved by my husband.

After Monkey's death, Tokugawa Ieyasu (Yasu) took the rule of Japan. She was sixty-five when Yasu became the first shogun of Tokugawa. According to her recently discovered real grave at Daitoku Temple in North-ward, Kyoto, Kicho lived thirteen more years and died peacefully at seventy-eight, in July, 1612. Daikoku Temple's hydrangea bush had purple flowers.

Yasu's Tokugawa Shogunate lasted for two hundred and fifty more years, as did peace in Japan.

(end)

---

[83] There is a record which says Lord Tea-whisk gave Kicho money. Wikipedia. He and Hide were allies.

Author's Note

The characters of Kano and Kicho were created but the documented historical facts and common beliefs are not. There have been many speculations, but the reason why Akechi Mitsuhide carried out the hopeless coup still remains a mystery. If he, an intelligent man, believed he would succeed, why was he so confident? If, on the other hand, he knowingly took an enormous risk, what did compel him to do so?

Reading historical records including recently discovered facts, I was astounded that past historians completely ignored Lady Nobunaga. For example, Kicho was with Nobunaga, according to Akechi chronicle, at the Joubodaiin Temple on the eve of the honorable return to Gifu after re-establishing the Ashikaga Shogunate. Ota Gyuichi, the author of Lord Nobunaga chronicle, omitted this important fact. As a woman, I wonder if it was purposely done.

Was it done because Ota Gyuichi was, then, employed by Toyotomi Hideyoshi who benefited from the coup? If the later rulers including Tokugawa Ieyasu tended to undermine the role of the lady, why? I feel that she held a secret which we will never know.

* * *

帰蝶は胸のあわせから父の懐剣をとり出した。刺繍を施した絹織物のさやは、父の匂いがした。お会いしたい。

帰蝶は懐剣を胸に抱いていたが、さやから抜き取り刃先を調べた。やがて首を左右に振り泣き崩れた。

帰蝶と信長（小紋寿ルミ）より。

Rumi Komonz (小紋寿ルミ) is a screen/pen name of the author Rumiko Commons who was born in Nihonbashi, Tokyo, Japan. She was a student hosted by the Rotary Club of Melbourne in '73-'74. She lives in Melbourne with her husband of 30 years, an engineer and a former champion triple jumper Don Commons, and two young adult children. B.A. Gakushuin '78, Dip Ed Monash '79, LLB La Trobe '07.

a Japanese website: http://p.booklog.jp/users/rumikomonz